The new catcher

Nick could actually hear himself breathing, even though he didn't feel as if he'd heard a lot from Coach Williams since he'd said "varsity catcher."

"Anyway," the coach said, "I just wanted to come over and tell you myself that you're going to have to play up for now."

Nick noticed for the first time that the coach was small for a grown-up, taller than Nick but not by a lot, with blond hair and a young face.

Nick said, "You still want me after seeing a throw like that?"

Coach Williams put his hand on Nick's shoulder. "Anybody can teach you control, son," he said. "God has to give you an arm like that."

"But I thought there was a rule at Hayworth that says you can't play varsity sports until eighth grade," Nick said. Almost sounding like he was trying to talk the coach out of it.

He saw that Coach Williams was smiling again.

"Not anymore," he said.

OTHER BOOKS YOU MAY ENJOY

SAFE AT HOME

a Comeback Kids novel

MIKE LUPICA

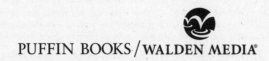

PUFFIN BOOKS / WALDEN MEDIA®

PUFFIN BOOKS

Published by the Penguin Group

Penguin Young Readers Group, 345 Hudson Street, New York, New York 10014, U.S.A.

Penguin Group (Canada), 90 Eglinton Avenue East, Suite 700,

Toronto, Ontario, Canada M4P 2Y3 (a division of Pearson Penguin Canada Inc.)

Penguin Books Ltd, 80 Strand, London WC2R 0RL, England

Penguin Ireland, 25 St Stephen's Green, Dublin 2, Ireland

(a division of Penguin Books Ltd)

Penguin Group (Australia), 250 Camberwell Road, Camberwell, Victoria 3124, Australia

(a division of Pearson Australia Group Pty Ltd)

Penguin Books India Pvt Ltd, 11 Community Centre,

Panchsheel Park, New Delhi - 110 017, India

Penguin Group (NZ), 67 Apollo Drive, Rosedale, North Shore 0632, New Zealand

(a division of Pearson New Zealand Ltd)

Penguin Books (South Africa) (Pty) Ltd, 24 Sturdee Avenue,

Rosebank, Johannesburg 2196, South Africa

Registered Offices: Penguin Books Ltd, 80 Strand, London WC2R 0RL, England

First published in the United States of America by Philomel Books,
a division of Penguin Young Readers Group, 2008
Published by Puffin Books, a division of Penguin Young Readers Group, 2009

This book is published in partnership with Walden Media, LLC. Walden Media and the
Walden Media skipping stone logo are trademarks and registered trademarks of Walden
Media LLC, 17 New England Executive Park, Bldg. 17, Suite 305, Burlington, MA 01803

9 10

Copyright © Mike Lupica, 2008
All rights reserved

THE LIBRARY OF CONGRESS HAS CATALOGED THE PHILOMEL EDITION AS FOLLOWS:
Lupica, Mike. Safe at home: a Comeback Kids novel / Mike Lupica. p. cm.
Summary: Playing baseball was the one thing that made twelve-year-old
Nick Crandall feel at home until he found acceptance with adoptive parents,
but he faces a new struggle to fit in when he becomes the first seventh-grader
ever to make the varsity baseball team.
ISBN: 978-0-399-24716-3 (hc)
[1. Baseball—Fiction. 2. Self-confidence—Fiction. 3. Teamwork (Sports)—Fiction.
4. Schools—Fiction. 5. Orphans—Fiction. 6. Adoption—Fiction.] I. Title.
PZ7.L97914Saf 2008 [Fic]—dc22 2007042100

Puffin Books ISBN 978-0-14-241460-6

Text set in Bookman.

Printed in the United States of America

Except in the United States of America, this book is sold subject to the condition that
it shall not, by way of trade or otherwise, be lent, re-sold, hired out, or otherwise
circulated without the publisher's prior consent in any form of binding or cover
other than that in which it is published and without a similar condition
including this condition being imposed on the subsequent purchaser.

The publisher does not have any control over and does not assume
any responsibility for author or third-party Web sites or their content.

Once again, for Taylor. And for Christopher and Alex and Zach and the real Gracie, our Hannah Grace. There isn't a single time I walk through the front door when I don't feel like the luckiest guy in the world.

ACKNOWLEDGMENTS

For Commissioner Nicholas Scoppetta of the New York City Fire Department, a foster-care child who never believed his dreams were out of reach.

And all those at New Yorkers For Children who were so generous with their time, and wisdom.

ONE

More than anything, Nick Crandall's real family had always been baseball.

He'd always felt that way about the teams he'd played on, since his first T-ball team. And he felt that way about the teams in the majors he followed, usually the ones with the best catchers, because Nick was a catcher, too.

Baseball was the only thing that made Nick feel like he really belonged. There were a lot of reasons why he loved baseball season, but that was the biggest.

Maybe everybody else on junior varsity at the Hayworth School, all the other sixth- and seventh-graders on the team, looked at the calendar and thought the school year was coming to an end.

Not Nick.

As far as he was concerned, everything was just beginning.

School baseball was for the spring, and that was his *only* team in the spring, because Paul and Brenda Crandall had one rule about sports: one team per season. Even that was all right with Nick. He got to play school ball every day except on the weekends, and he could look forward to playing in their town's summer Little League from the end of June into August.

So when *he* looked at the calendar, all he could see was baseball, practically all the way until school started again in the fall.

It was the first week of tryouts for JV, even though hardly anybody thought of them as *tryout* tryouts, because everybody who came out made the team. Some guys did get cut off varsity, made up of eighth- and ninth-graders, depending on how many came out. But even those guys, no matter how old they were, got moved down to JV if they still wanted to play.

Nobody moved up, though.

You didn't get to play varsity at Hayworth until

you were in eighth. Nobody was sure if it was an official written-down rule. But if you played sports at Hayworth, and everybody had to play at least one, you knew that's how things were done.

Nick didn't care. No *way* did he care. He was in no rush to play varsity, anyway. The varsity catcher, Bobby Mazzilli, was graduating with the rest of his class in June. So in Nick's mind, a mind filled with baseball stuff the way his desk drawers were filled with baseball cards and magazines, next year he had a good shot at being varsity catcher.

That was no sure thing, of course, even though things seemed to be set up just right for him. Because more than anything he knew about baseball, Nick knew this:

There were no sure things in your life.

For now, Nick was happy on JV. Most of this year's team was made up of seventh-graders, which meant that Nick knew all of them from class, whether they were in his homeroom or not, Hayworth not being *that* big a school.

None of the guys on the team were what he thought of as real friends, just because that was a small category for him, wherever he'd gone to school. For now, Nick Crandall had only two real friends in the whole world.

And one was a girl, not that Nick would ever admit that to the other seventh-grade boys, actually admit having a girl as one of his best buds.

The girl was Gracie Wright, also a seventh-grader at Hayworth. Not only was she in his home-room, she lived directly across the street from Nick and took the same bus and spent about as much time in the Crandall house as he spent in hers.

His other bud—not quite up there with Gracie, but close enough—was Jack Elmore, an eighth-grader. Jack was fourteen, and Nick hadn't even turned thirteen yet. His birthday was still a couple of months away, officially making him the young-est seventh-grader at Hayworth. That official-type information came from Gracie, who pretty much knew everything about the kids at their school as far as Nick could tell.

But what even Gracie, as much of a know-it-all as she could be sometimes, didn't know was how truly fast things could change in baseball, when you least expected them to.

And how fast they were going to change for Nick today.

The JV practiced on the last of the upper fields at Hayworth, the one with the best view of the soccer and lacrosse fields below. The varsity practiced *way* closer to the white classroom buildings and had the best-taken-care-of field at their school, one with a real dirt infield and a working scoreboard and even bleachers behind both benches, where parents could sit to watch games.

Nick had been stealing looks at the varsity practice all afternoon. At one point, he noticed a big crowd of players at home plate and thought they might actually be quitting early today, even though they were usually still on the field when the JV packed it in for the day.

Soon after that, Nick spotted the varsity coach, Coach Williams, leaning against a tree down the left-field line of the JV field, hanging there by himself in the shade.

Watching them.

"What's *he* doing there?" Zach Dugas, their third baseman, said as he stepped to the plate.

The JV version of the Hayworth Tigers was scrimmaging by now, using just two outfielders—there were still only fifteen players on the team, total, until they found out about varsity cuts—and their coach, Mr. Leeman, was doing the pitching for both teams.

"Don't know," Nick said. "Maybe he just likes baseball so much he'll watch any game. Even one of ours that doesn't count."

"Doubtful," Zach said.

Jeff Kantor was the runner at first, having just singled, and there were two outs, which meant to Nick that Jeff was going to be running, even with Mr. Leeman pitching from the stretch.

Everybody was encouraged to run by the coach. He'd told them from the first day of practice they were going to be the runningest team in their league.

Probably running on the first pitch, Nick thought.

Bad idea.

Really bad.

It wasn't something he'd ever say out loud. When you'd spent your whole life trying to fit in, trying to please people, trying so hard to be one of the guys, the *last* thing you wanted to do was sound cocky. Or sound like you were big-timing anybody.

But facts were facts. Four runners already had tried to steal today—tried *Nick*—and he had thrown out all four of them.

He couldn't help wondering now if Coach Williams of the varsity had seen any of those babies, especially the one that had Ollie Brown by so much at second base that Ollie didn't even bother to slide.

In the language of baseball announcers, all of whom felt like members of Nick's baseball family, like funny uncles he'd never met, he had thrown absolute *peas* all three times.

"Frozen peas," according to Zach, who'd been Nick's first victim when he'd been rock-headed enough to try to steal third on him in the first inning.

Everybody knew by now what kind of player Nick was. The rest of the seventh-graders knew he could hit, knew he could run for a catcher, even as stocky as he was, with those short, thick legs that he kept hoping would grow one of these days.

Even at twelve, he could locate a pop foul behind the plate with the best of them, toss his mask away and actually catch the ball, something hardly anybody his age could do.

Like he had some kind of radar tracking system going for him, what Gracie said was like some chip he had inside his body somewhere.

Yet that wasn't what set Nick Crandall apart on a ballfield. What set him apart was the way he could throw from behind the plate.

Nick Crandall had an arm on him.

He'd always been able to throw, even on the playgrounds, back when he was living in Riverdale, in the Bronx in New York City. But last year was the first year he'd really been able to show it off. From the first few days of tryouts last year, when Coach Leeman had asked for volunteers to catch and that right arm of Nick's had shot straight up in the air, he could see how shocked everybody was when he erased another runner as if he'd hit the Delete key on his computer.

"Dude," Ollie Brown had said to him today, after Nick had schooled him so badly on his stolen-base attempt. "Guys our age aren't supposed to get thrown out by that much unless they do a *header* between first and second."

Throwing out guys stealing was Nick's very best thing. He didn't get all the runners who tried him. Even Johnny Bench, the old Cincinnati Red from the Big Red Machine, who Nick had read up on and who was supposed to be the best defensive catcher of all time, didn't come close to doing that.

Sometimes Nick would bounce one.

Sometimes he'd throw wild left or wild right.

Sometimes, as if he didn't know his own strength, he'd *really* let one fly and the ball would go sailing in the direction of Dave Chester, their center fielder, known as Junior on their team because he looked so much like Ken Griffey, Jr.

Most of the time, though, Nick was money.

And he had been money today.

The safest Nick felt in his life, the most confident and sure of himself, the most normal, was when he'd hear one of his teammates yell "he's going!" just as he saw the runner take off from first, and then he'd be coming up and out of his crouch, and his arm would be coming forward, and he would be the no-worries Nick Crandall he wanted to be more than anything.

That was the way it was happening now as Coach Leeman brought his arm forward and delivered his first pitch to Zach. It wasn't any kind of pitch-out, the kind that big-league catchers would call to give them a better chance if they thought a guy was about to steal, a pitch they'd have the pitcher purposely throw high and way off the plate so they'd be standing and ready to throw as soon as they came out from behind the batter to catch it.

It might as well have been.

Coach Leeman's pitch just happened to be high and wide, and that could have been a problem if Nick hadn't read it perfectly almost from the time it came out of Coach's hand. As Nick straightened up to catch the ball, he could see that Jeff, one of their fastest guys on the bases, hadn't gotten nearly a good enough jump.

If Coach Williams hadn't seen the other throws, he was sure going to see one now.

Nick really leaned into this one and cut it loose, grunting loudly as he did.

The moment the ball came out of his hand, he

knew he had put too much on it. *Way* too much. And he knew why, knew it the way you knew you'd said something wrong the second the words were out of your mouth, when it was too late to take them back: because he was a dope trying to show off for the varsity coach.

To Nick's eyes, the ball was still rising like a plane taking off as it went over second base, over the head of Reed McDonagh, playing short for Nick's team, and over the head of the sliding runner. It was still so high in the sky that Nick was suddenly afraid that the ball might make it all the way to center field on the fly.

Junior wound up fielding the throw on one bounce and didn't even bother trying to get Jeff at third. There was no chance, so he just threw the ball back in to Reed at second. As he did, Nick heard Zach Dugas, in a real loud voice, saying, "I was starting to worry that sucker was going to need one of those parachutes you see on rockets after reentry."

Nick didn't say anything. He was too embarrassed. He didn't mind getting people's attention with his arm. But you never ever wanted to draw attention to yourself like this. He was used to messing up in his life. Sometimes the messing up was epic, too.

More than anything he hated to do that in baseball.

He took off his mask finally, just because it gave him something to do. Then he walked slowly back around the plate, taking long enough that it felt like he was taking a walk around the block, and yelled out to his fielders to remember there were still two out.

Then he got into his crouch and watched from there as Zach beat the next pitch into the ground and Reed at least showed off a strong *accurate* arm by throwing him out from deep short.

It was then that Nick saw Coach Williams walking in from where he'd been standing in foul territory, walking past third base now, straight down the faded white line between third and home.

Walking straight toward Nick.

Yeah, Nick thought, he probably can't wait for me to be his catcher next season.

As Coach Williams got closer, Nick could see that he was smiling, slowly shaking his head.

Great. He'd cracked up the varsity baseball coach.

Coach Williams was still smiling when he got to home plate and was standing where a right-handed batter would stand, right there in front of Nick.

"That was some throw," he said.

Nick put his head down. "I usually have better control than that."

Now Coach Williams laughed. "Well, I *hope* so."

"Really, Coach, I do."

"I know," he said. "It's Nick, right?"

"Yes, sir," he said, "Nick Crandall."

He put out his hand the way he'd been taught by Paul Crandall and looked Coach Williams in the eye as the two of them shook hands, Nick thinking, My hand is almost as big as his.

Then Coach Williams said, "I just wanted to officially meet my new varsity catcher."

Nick wasn't big on surprises. He'd had enough of those already to last him the rest of his life.

A few good surprises.

Mostly bad.

"I don't understand," he said to Coach Williams.

"Bobby Mazzilli broke a bone in his wrist today on a play at the plate. His mom just called from the hospital," he said.

"How?" Nick said.

"He was being a catcher, even in preseason," Coach Williams said. "Blocked the plate like a champ, Les Roy flattened him, and both of them fell on his right wrist. He's gonna be fine, but he's gonna miss a chunk of the season. How much depends on how fast or slow he heals. For now, all we know is that he's in a soft cast."

Nick could actually hear himself breathing, even though he didn't feel as if he'd heard a lot from Coach Williams since he'd said "varsity catcher."

"Anyway," the coach said, "I just wanted to come over and tell you myself that you're going to have to play up for now."

Nick noticed for the first time that the coach was small for a grown-up, taller than Nick but not by a lot, with blond hair and a young face.

Nick said, "You still want me after seeing a throw like that?"

Coach Williams put his hand on Nick's shoulder. "Anybody can teach you control, son," he said. "God has to give you an arm like that."

"But I thought there was a rule at Hayworth that says you can't play varsity sports until eighth grade," Nick said. Almost sounding like he was trying to talk the coach out of it.

He saw that Coach Williams was smiling again.

"Not anymore," he said.

TWO

The rest of practice was a blur. So was the ride home with Brenda Crandall, his mom. He didn't tell her about varsity when she asked about his day, thinking that he would wait and tell both her and his dad when they were having dinner.

In his heart, though, he knew differently.

Something this big, he had to tell Gracie Wright first.

Nick would never admit this to anybody, especially not Gracie, who'd just make fun of him if he did, but she was the person he trusted the most. And she was the person he most wanted to be like, even if she was a girl.

It didn't mean that he wanted to grow up and be like her, the way he wanted to grow up and be one of the best catchers in baseball, be Joe Mauer of the Twins or Russell Martin of the Dodgers, his new favorites.

It wasn't that she was so much smarter than he was. Nick was smart, too, though it wasn't like he had the grades to prove it these days, and he was starting to hear about that from his teachers and from his parents. *Especially* his parents, who just happened to be teachers themselves. It was the way Gracie was smart.

She was smart about people.

But the thing that he liked the most in Gracie, the big one, was that she wasn't afraid.

Gracie was brave.

On top of that, she had never seemed to give a rip that Nick was adopted.

Nick had told her he was adopted the first day he met her, maybe a half hour after she'd come across the street and rung the Crandalls' doorbell and introduced herself, the day after they'd moved into town and moved into this neighborhood.

"We're gonna be friends," Gracie had said when they were on the swings in her backyard. "So I'm gonna need to know some stuff about you."

She asked what his parents did, and he told her they were college professors, English for his dad, math for his mom. Then she wanted to know where he had grown up.

And that's where it always got tricky for Nick, because where he'd grown up hadn't been around here and hadn't been with the Crandalls, and so he'd just blurted it out.

"I'm adopted," he said.

And Gracie had smiled at him—Nick could still see her smiling that smile now—and said, "I'm a soccer player."

She was. Soccer and lacrosse were her best sports.

"No, I mean it," Nick had said. "I didn't even get adopted until I was nine, which I think is some kind of world record."

"Okaaaaay," Gracie had said. "But we're still gonna be friends and so don't try to get out of it."

And pretty much from that moment, that is exactly what they had been.

Even when he wanted to be alone, as much as he had felt alone for most of his life, it hardly ever meant being alone from Gracie.

Gracie Wright pretty much treated every day as if it was going to be the best day she'd ever have in her life.

Now they were back where they'd started that first day, in Gracie's backyard, sitting on the swings, even though they both had really had outgrown them.

Gracie was the same height as Nick, with brown hair that was already starting to get streaked by the sun now that she was outdoors every day playing lacrosse. Right now, most of that hair was covered up by her favorite sports cap, one with the Dallas Mavericks logo on front. Gracie wasn't a big Mavericks fan. She just liked the colors and the way the *M* looked.

"Only you," she said, "could act as if getting called up to varsity, for however long it lasts, is a *bad* thing."

"I didn't say it was a bad thing."

"Did."

"Did not," Nick said. "What I *said* was, it was a surprise. And you know how I feel about surprises."

"Ooooooh," Gracie said, "surprises," and covered up her head like the sky was about to fall on it. "Surprises are soooo scary!"

"Can I just say one thing without you making fun of me?" Nick said.

Gracie smiled. "I *suppose* I could do that, just this once."

"I was happy on JV, is all," he said. "It wasn't like I was looking for the varsity to come along and adopt me."

"You're not getting adopted, gumball," Gracie said. "You're getting *promoted*."

"Well, it doesn't feel that way."

"Baseball is your best thing. You're the best catcher your age around, and you ought to be on varsity, whether you're in seventh or not. Even if it doesn't turn out to be the whole season, think about what great experience you'll get."

"I'm worried that I'm gonna get up there and stink," he said. "That's what I think my experience is gonna be."

Gracie gave him a little shove, a playful one, her way of letting him know that whatever she said next wasn't going to be mean.

She said, "Well, there's a surprise, you worrying about something."

"What's that supposed to mean?"

"You know exactly what that's supposed to mean. Sometimes you're better at worrying than you are at whipping a baseball around." She wagged a finger at him now. "But you just wait. One of these days you're gonna figure out that even with the bad stuff that's happened to you, it's gonna be all good for you from now on. Things are going to turn out for you the way they do in your comic books."

It was one more thing about Nick that Gracie knew, something hardly anybody else in the world knew: how much he loved comic books. Not as much as baseball. He knew other kids his age would rather be on their laptops all the time, or playing video games. Nick liked that stuff, too. He just liked his comic books more.

Gracie was right. Things usually did come out the way he wanted them to in his comics.

"You know I'm right," Gracie said.

"You always are," Nick said. "At least that's what you're always telling me."

"Yeah, Crandall, I know I am," she said in a softer voice, not her funny-Gracie voice. "But this time I'm *really* right."

Nick smiled now. Sometimes he couldn't help it when he was with Gracie, no matter what they were talking about. A smile would come out of him when he least expected it, like a rabbit popping out of a hat.

No matter how much worry he'd brought with him across the street.

She was right about varsity, and Nick knew she was. Making varsity, even this way, because somebody got hurt, wasn't anything like being adopted, and that was something Nick was smarter about than Gracie Wright, something he knew better than anybody.

Better than he wanted to.

It wasn't just that he'd been adopted once already in his life. It had nearly happened twice.

THREE

Nick had always known as much as he was allowed to about how he came to be a foster child.

The grown-ups in his life, the ones who'd taken care of him until the Crandalls had adopted him right after his ninth birthday, told him that when he was older he could find out who his birth parents were if he really wanted to, could get the names of the people who had given up their "parental rights" when he was born.

Nick wasn't sure what he thought about that or what he'd do when he was older, mostly because he was having enough trouble with being young. He told himself that was something he'd be able to worry about later—as Gracie liked to tell him, his plate was full enough with worry for now.

He just knew that from the time he could really

remember stuff, his foster parents had been Mr. and Mrs. Boyd, Bob and Diane Boyd. He knew there had been another set of foster parents before that, up until he was three or so. But no matter how hard Nick tried, he couldn't remember them.

The Boyds were older than regular parents—Nick could see that from the time he started preschool in Riverdale. They were more like grandparents, really, when you compared them to the other parents Nick saw at school.

Nick had never called Mr. and Mrs. Boyd Mom or Dad. Instead he'd called them Poppa and Nana. They'd told him that as much as they loved him and would always love him, maybe in a way he wouldn't understand until he was older—something else he'd know when he was older—they were just raising him until he got adopted for good, by "adoptive parents."

So it didn't take Nick long in his life to figure out something: If you started out your life in foster care, there were a whole bunch of different ways they had, a bunch of different adjectives they used, to describe parents.

Birth parents.

Foster parents.

Adoptive parents.

"When will I get adopted?" Nick used to ask the Boyds, probably more than he should have.

And usually it was Nana who would hug him and tell him, "Soon as somebody knows how special you are, the way we do. The way we did the first day we brought you to this apartment."

Nick kept waiting for that to happen.

And waiting.

And waiting.

Then, when he was seven, he met Mr. and Mrs. Wells.

Nick was sure it was going to happen with Mr. and Mrs. Wells, from the day the Boyds had told him there was a couple that wanted to meet him.

"A *young* couple," Mr. Boyd had said, "not a couple of old goats like us."

First Nick met them at the Boyds' apartment on Elm Street. The next meeting was at what was called a "neutral site," an expression Nick had only heard in sports before then. In this case, the neutral site turned out to be the Westchester County Mall up in White Plains, not so far from where Mr. and Mrs. Wells lived in Connecticut.

Next Nick got to spend a whole day with the Wellses, and the day included a trip to Shea Stadium to watch the Mets play. When Nick thought back on it now, he knew that was the day he really fell in love with baseball, not just because it was his first trip to a real big-league ballpark, but because it was all wrapped up in how sure he was that he was going to spend the rest of his life as Nick Wells.

Nick could still remember everything about that Sunday-afternoon game between the Mets and the Braves at Shea. Just about every seat in the old place was filled, because the Mets and Braves were big rivals fighting for first place that year. The Mets' colors were blue and orange, but what Nick remembered the very best was how once he'd come through the turnstiles and up some ramps and past the concession stands and then into the amazingly bright ballpark sun, there was the green grass. It seemed to stretch in all directions, until the bright blue outfield walls got in the way in the distance.

They had tremendous seats that day, five rows behind the Mets dugout. Not only did all the action seem as if it were right in front of him, close enough to reach out and touch, it was also as if Nick were *hearing* baseball for the first time. Or at least in a way he never had before, hearing the pop of the ball in the catcher's mitt and the knock of the ball on a wood bat, sounds Nick had never heard in person before. When a hitter really connected on a pitch, it was as if a firecracker had gone off right next to him.

It was a great game, back and forth the whole day, the Mets leading, and then the Braves leading, and the Mets finally tying them in the bottom of the ninth. At that point it became a perfect day for Nick, because the game went into extra innings, and a day that he never wanted to end wasn't over yet.

Sitting there behind the dugout, trying to keep score the way Mr. Wells had shown him, wearing the Mets cap Mr. Wells had bought for him at one of the souvenir stands, Nick didn't know what he wanted more, for the Mets to win or for the game to keep going.

The Mets finally did win, in the bottom of the thirteenth inning on a Mike Piazza home run, the Mets catcher having enough left to hit one out even after catching all those innings. When the ball cleared the left-field wall by a mile and ended up in what Mr. Wells explained was the "picnic area" out there, Nick stood and yelled his head off with the rest of the 50,000 fans.

But even as he did, there was a part of him that almost felt like crying, because the game being over meant that it was time for him to leave, time for him to go back to the apartment on Elm Street in Riverdale.

For a few hours, though, Nick had finally found two places where he knew he belonged:

A ballpark and in that seat in the fifth row between Mr. and Mrs. Wells.

He turned out to be half right.

The next step was supposed to be a sleepover at their house in Connecticut.

Nick never made it to Connecticut, at least not that time.

The night before he was supposed to go, Nick carefully packed his duffel bag. Not just with the clothes he was going to wear, but his catcher's mitt as well, because Mr. Wells said they were going to play a *lot* of catch.

And his Mets cap, which he'd pretty much been wearing nonstop since he'd gotten back from Shea Stadium.

As they had left the ballpark that day, people still clapping and cheering and yelling on their way out of Shea and into the parking lots, Mr. Wells had told him not to worry—adults had been telling him that his whole life—that there were going to be a lot of trips to the ballpark like this.

Except that morning he was supposed to go on the sleepover, he could tell something was wrong when he came down to breakfast, could see it in the faces of Mr. and Mrs. Boyd.

Then they sat him down and explained that the Wellses had changed their minds.

Nick didn't cry in front of them, sitting between them on the living room couch, as much as he wanted to.

He just said, "What did I do wrong?"

Mrs. Boyd hugged him then, though Nick didn't feel much like being hugged, and said, "Honey, you didn't do anything wrong. They just decided they want to adopt a newborn baby, if they can find one."

Nick said, "Nobody wanted *me* when I was a baby, and nobody wants me now," and ran to his room.

He cried there, spent the day in there with his comic books inside the world where things came out the way you wanted them to, even more than they did in baseball.

He still loved baseball after that. Couldn't *not* love baseball. And he still rooted for the Mets. And on TV when they'd show some foul ball landing behind the Mets dugout, he'd be able to pick out almost exactly where he had been sitting between Mr. and Mrs. Wells.

It just wasn't the perfect memory it was supposed to be. He'd been back to Shea a few times since, and as much as he remembered the magic of that first time, the smells of the place and the sounds of the place and even all the green made him remember something else:

Being sent back to foster care.

• • •

After that, Nick was convinced that he could wait forever and never get adopted. It turned out he didn't even have to wait a year. A few months later, they used his story on one of the "Wednesday's Child" segments on Channel 4. Nick didn't know anything about it until the reporter and the cameraman came to the Boyds' apartment and interviewed him and Mr. and Mrs. Boyd, but it was some kind of series they ran on boys and girls still waiting to be adopted.

Nick didn't know what to think about that, because he'd never told any of the kids at his school in Riverdale that he was in foster care in the first place.

But it was summer and school was out, and Poppa and Nana Boyd told him it was a good thing.

They were right.

The very next week, Paul and Brenda Crandall—old but not as old as the Boyds—were sitting in the apartment on Elm Street and having their first meeting with Nick. Then there was another meeting. And a trip to the city to visit the Museum of Natural History with all the dinosaurs, what had to be the biggest and best and coolest dino exhibit in the whole world.

Nick made it to the sleepover this time, made it all the way to Connecticut.

When the adoption was finalized, after Nick had met with all the social workers and counselors and the nice people from the Administration for Children's Services, Nick had said to Mr. and Mrs. Crandall, "What should I call you?"

He thought Mrs. Crandall was going to cry as she said, "Mom. And Dad."

Nick said, "Are you sure?"

She said, "As sure as we've been of anything in our lives."

"It took so long," Nick had said to her that day.

"For us, too," she'd said. "But we had to find the exact right boy. And now we have."

Mr. Crandall had said, "I've taught English pretty much my whole life, Nick. And I can tell you something from experience: Story is everything. And now your story is finally going to have the happy ending it deserves."

"Even if this ending is really just a beginning," Mrs. Crandall said.

Nick knew by then that they had tried and tried to have a child of their own and never could. Late in life, at least late to be parents, they had decided all over again how much they still wanted to have one.

"We'd given up," she'd said. "But then one day we decided that you should never give up on your dreams. That's when we saw you on TV."

"My dream was just to get adopted," Nick had said. "But then I sort of gave up on ever finding adoptive parents."

"No," Brenda Crandall said. And then she started to cry, and Nick thought he'd done something wrong, said something to make her this sad. He just didn't know what.

"I'm sorry," he said.

"Don't be sorry," she said. "These are happy tears."

Then Mrs. Crandall told him he didn't have to put any words in front of *parents* ever again.

"We're just your parents," she said.

FOUR

Nick had finally found parents.

They just happened to be parents who knew hardly anything about baseball. Instead they were parents who wanted him to be as good in school as he was in baseball.

They tried to understand baseball. They really did. Nick could see his mom, especially, really trying, and he appreciated that she knew a lot more now than when they'd first adopted him, when she basically didn't know a fair ball from a foul ball.

The first time she'd seen him play a game, she'd had only one question afterward:

"If the position you play isn't dangerous, how come you're the only one out there who has to wear equipment?"

Nick didn't take it personally. He just figured that you were either a sports fan or you weren't. And the Crandalls weren't. They seemed to be in great shape for people their age, though. They liked to take long walks after dinner, and both Nick and his dad liked to take bike rides together. That was when the two of them seemed to do their best talking. And sometimes when there was a baseball game on television that Nick wanted to watch and his dad wasn't doing anything, Paul Crandall the English professor would sit on the couch with Nick and ask him questions.

Just the fact that he was making the effort meant a lot to Nick.

It was why Nick would try to act interested when Paul Crandall would start talking about books, like reading wasn't his job but his favorite sport. Nick didn't even try to explain that the only books he really cared about were his comic books.

Comic books were about adventure and about heroes who weren't afraid of danger or anything else, *super*heroes who could overcome anything and anybody, no matter where they came from or what bad things had happened to them in their lives. They could beat the odds and the bad guys and always end up feeling like winners.

Sometimes Nick wished he were living in a comic book world, even now that he had parents.

They weren't exactly the parents he'd always imagined for himself. Nick had to be honest about that, at least with himself. It wasn't so much with his mom as with his dad. In Nick's dreams, his happy-ending dreams, he'd always imagined himself being adopted by a dad who wanted to go outside and throw a ball around with him, who wanted to take him to ballgames and maybe coach him in Little League and watch baseball on television—for fun, not because he felt he had to.

Now he had Paul Crandall, who would rather talk about books than baseball but would shake his head when he'd see Nick with his head buried in one of his comic books.

So this was one more thing for Nick to worry about, that maybe his dad had imagined a different kind of son for himself, one who wasn't into sports the way Nick was, one who didn't come home covered with dirt and bumps and bruises.

Things definitely weren't great right now with his dad, no getting around that. Nick was doing worse in school than he ever had. And the more he struggled in class, the more he only wanted to read comic books, not schoolbooks.

He could see all this making his dad more and more disappointed with him, as angry about Nick's study habits and his grades as he ever got about anything, especially as Nick got closer to the end of the school year and his final grades.

"We're not going to threaten you with taking away school baseball," Paul Crandall had said the other day. "You've only got so many baseball seasons to play, and we've only got so many to watch you play. But you have to do better in school, and not just in English. Your work in math, let's face it, has been even worse this year."

His mother the math teacher wasn't there at the time, so Nick wasn't afraid to say, "The only thing I hate more than math is math *homework*."

Paul Crandall almost managed a smile. "Nobody except your mother loves math," he said. "But that's not the point. The point is that you can do better in it with some effort. Ask yourself a question, Nick: How can you memorize all those base-ball stats and figure out someone's batting average yet *not* be able to solve simple equations?"

"I love baseball, that's why, more than I'll ever love school," he said. "And that's another thing about me that's never going to change, no matter how hard you try."

Saying that even though Paul and Brenda Crandall had devoted their whole lives to school.

"That's not the point," Paul Crandall said. "School is about results the same as baseball is. And if we don't see some with your final grades, I'm not making any promises about summer base-ball this year."

"It's not going to make me care more about school," Nick said, digging in.

"Fine," Paul Crandall said. "But your mother and I *do* care."

They'd been having the conversation in Nick's room. Paul Crandall got up then and walked out, tell-ing him to get to work on that night's homework.

Leaving Nick with one more thing to worry about, maybe the biggest worry he had, that maybe neither he nor his parents had gotten exactly what they were looking for.

For now, though, at dinner, he was trying to explain to them what it meant to be moved up to varsity from the seventh grade.

"Sounds to me like quite an honor," Paul Crandall said. "Almost as if you've graduated from junior varsity early. We're proud of you, Nick."

"Well, I haven't actually *done* anything yet," Nick said. "It's more like I got called up from the minors, for the time being, anyway. Even Coach isn't sure how long this might last."

Brenda Crandall, wanting to join in, said, "Well, technically, aren't all of you boys minors?"

"No, no," Nick said. "It's a baseball expression. In pro ball, there's the minor leagues, where guys go when they're first starting out, and then there's the majors, which is where the best guys end up eventually."

It was like this a lot at the dinner table when the conversation turned to sports. Nick acted like he was the professor and they were the students.

"Sort of like undergrads and graduate students, dear," Paul Crandall said to his wife. "I believe there are some pro teams around Connecticut, aren't there, Nick? Including one down in Bridgeport?"

Nick wondered if it was something he'd learned in one of his late-night baseball quizzes.

"There are," Nick said. "Our class got to go to a game last year, remember? They've got this cool little ballpark near the water."

Paul Crandall smiled and said, "The Bluefish, I believe they're called." Now he really was like a kid in class with the right answer, and clearly pleased with himself.

Nick reached over and offered his hand for a high five, and Paul Crandall, looking a little uncomfortable doing it, managed to give him one back.

"Way to go, Dad," Nick said.

Brenda Crandall said to Nick, "Now you're sure you're all right with this move, really?"

"I guess so."

"You don't sound too enthusiastic."

Nick said, "It's just that I knew everybody on the JV team, and the only guy I know on the varsity is Jack Elmore. I was talking to him online before, and even though he *said* he thought guys on the varsity would be cool with me playing with them, he wasn't really sure."

"It's a surprise," Brenda Crandall said, "isn't it?"

It was as if his mom had hit the jackpot. "It's a surprise," Nick said.

"You know," she said, "surprises can be good sometimes."

It just turned out to be one more thing she didn't know about baseball.

FIVE

Coach Williams called all the varsity players around him before practice and told them that Nick was going to be their new catcher until Bobby came back and that nobody, not even Bobby's doctors, knew when that would be.

Nick looked around at all the different faces. It wasn't as if Coach had told them that they were all going for ice cream after practice.

"Listen, we thought we had our starting team, but injuries happen in sports," he said. "So now the team we start the season with—and maybe play the whole season with, depending on Bobby—is the one that has Nick behind the plate."

Nobody said anything until Gary Watson, the star pitcher for the Hayworth Tigers, said, "Bobby's the only catcher who's ever caught me."

Coach Williams said, "I understand that, Gary. But I'm sure it won't take long for you and Nick to get on the same page. And besides, even with Bobby, didn't you basically call your own game, anyway?"

"Well, not always."

Coach Williams grinned as if none of this was very big stuff. "And I don't want to risk offending my ace, but it's not as if we have to make a lot of decisions when you've got the ball in your hand. Fastballs in or fastballs away, am I right?"

"It's not that simple," Gary said.

Not letting it go.

Like he wanted to make an issue out of it.

Gary looked at Nick and then back at his coach and finally said, "He's a seventh-grader, Coach."

Nick thought, He makes it sound like a dirty word.

"And," Gary continued, "look at him. He might not be small for his age, but he's too small to catch for varsity. The first time there's a collision at home plate, somebody on the other team is going to knock him all the way to the backstop."

"Or through it," somebody said from behind Nick.

Another voice that Nick didn't recognize said, "His chest protector is almost as big as he is."

One more voice said, "Fits him like a dress."

There were some giggles.

"Any other equipment humor?" Coach Williams said, looking around.

It got their attention.

"Now I have something to say," he said. "If I didn't think this particular seventh-grader was big enough or good enough to play up and good enough to catch you and our other pitchers, he wouldn't be here even for one game."

Coach was still grinning as he said it. But his tone had changed. He was letting them all know who the coach was and who the players were, whether they were star players or not.

Now the biggest kid on the team raised his hand. Nick knew this was Steve Carberry, the team's first baseman. He wasn't just the biggest kid on the team, he was the biggest kid in the ninth grade at Hayworth.

"I used to catch in Little League," Steve said.

Coach Williams nodded. "Apparently," he said

to Steve, "that fact slipped your mind yesterday when I asked for volunteers to replace Bobby."

"But, Coach, I didn't know when you asked that—"

"Didn't know what?"

Steve looked uncomfortable—everybody was staring at him.

At least they've stopped staring at me for a second, Nick thought.

"Didn't know that you were gonna bring somebody up from JV."

JV, Nick thought. Another dirty word to these guys.

"And you have a problem with that?" Coach Williams said.

Steve looked down at his baseball shoes, which seemed huge to Nick, like man shoes. When he looked up again he said, "None of us got the chance to play up."

"None of you got to play up before *I* got here," Coach Williams said. "And if something like this had happened *after* I became the head coach here, it would have been you or Gary or somebody else I was walking over here from the JV field."

He looked to his left now, then his right, making it clear that he was about to address all of them at once. "We need to get to work," he said. "But if anybody else has any other objections to Nick being our catcher—any that make sense, anyway—let's hear them right now. Because this is the last time we're going to have this conversation as a group."

Nobody said anything.

Coach Williams turned to Nick. "Anything you'd like to say, Nick?" he said.

"I'll do my best" was the best he could do at the moment, in a voice small enough to fit in the pocket of his mitt.

"That's all we ask of anybody around here," the coach said. "Now, Gary, you and Nick go do some throwing on the side while we start infield."

The rest of the Hayworth Tigers went one way. Gary and Nick went another, though Nick could see Gary wasn't any happier about that than he was with Nick being on this field with him in the first place.

While infield practice went on, Gary pitched

to Nick, not putting anything on the ball at first, gradually letting his pitches pick up steam, until by the end he was bringing it with everything he had, almost as if he was hoping he could throw one fastball hard enough to knock Nick over.

If it had been one of the JV pitchers throwing this hard and this well, Nick would have been up every few pitches, even on the side, cheering him on.

Even though Gary Watson had made it clear he didn't want Nick here, Nick couldn't help thinking, as he caught one hard strike after another, that Gary was the best pitcher he'd caught in his life.

But he didn't say a word to Gary the whole time, and Gary didn't say a word to him.

The only sound on this side of the field was the pop of the ball, exploding, the unmistakable sound of a good fastball, in Nick's glove.

Usually a baseball field was the place where Nick felt most sure of himself, where he felt as if he was the one in control of things. When he'd get down behind home plate and look around, everybody was where they were supposed to be, things actually made sense.

Maybe not in the whole world—just the one spread out in front of him in the infield and outfield.

It had been that way from the first day he'd put on his mask and chest protector and knee pads.

Nick especially liked the mask. It wasn't just that it made him feel a little bit like a superhero from one of his comic books. The mask made him feel as if he could hide in plain sight, looking at everybody else's face on the field without them seeing his. After all the times when he'd worried about people looking at him, wondering if they were seeing the boy who didn't have real parents, wondering how many people really knew he was in foster care or adopted, Nick thought a mask wasn't such a bad thing to have handy.

Yet even his trusty mask couldn't help him today.

It was as if he'd forgotten how to catch or throw.

At one point his buddy Jack Elmore, the backup second baseman on the team, came up and whispered, "Is this your first day of varsity baseball or just your first day of baseball *period*?"

Jack wasn't as funny as Gracie, who seemed to Nick to have more of a grown-up sense of humor than a kid sense of humor. Still, Jack was pretty funny. Nick just didn't need him to be funny today, mostly because Nick's baseball was funny enough. The kid who didn't want other kids looking at him was making it almost impossible for them to look anywhere else.

Nick whispered back to Jack, "Is that your idea of having my back?"

Jack said, "Dude, I gotta be honest with you: You need more than me today."

Jack was right. Even before they had started scrimmaging, as Nick was trying to catch batting practice from Coach Williams, with Coach just grooving fat pitches for the hitters, the ball kept ticking off Nick's glove when guys would swing and miss. Or low pitches would skip through his legs no matter how hard he tried to block them, as if the space between his pads was suddenly as wide as the space between first base and third.

It grew even worse from there.

Because now he couldn't even throw.

It wasn't that he was throwing too far, the way

he had in front of the coach yesterday, when he'd uncorked the throw that looked as if it belonged in one of those Pass, Punt and Kick contests where guys would try to heave a football as far as they could. Nick *wished* it were only that.

No.

Today he was doing the worst thing you could do in sports—he was trying to be too careful. Because he was too afraid to make a mistake. And when you did that in sports, any sport, all you *did* was make mistakes. So on his first throw down to second, trying to get the guy stealing on him, he bounced the ball about ten feet in front of Joey Johnson, their shortstop, covering the base. When the runner, Chris Galuccio, decided to steal third on the next pitch, Nick tried to snap off a throw from his crouch, and the ball sailed so wide that even somebody standing in the third-base coach's box would have had a hard time making a play on it.

Gary Watson happened to be the batter. Now he said something loud enough for only Nick to hear, like it was just the two of them in the back of a class: "When you master throwing standing up, maybe then you can try it sitting down."

Nick ignored him, just took a couple of steps toward third base and yelled to Conor Bell, the team's third baseman, "My bad."

It made Gary Watson laugh. "Bad?" he said. "Bad is when you miss the base with a throw. You missed the whole stinking *field*, dude."

There was nothing for Nick to say back. Even if he had had Gracie there getting in his ear and telling him what to say, giving him some smart comeback, Nick knew he still wouldn't have said anything. He had read enough about sports to know how rookies were supposed to behave, how they were supposed to know their place.

How they were supposed to keep their mouths shut.

Nick did that now. As he walked past Gary and back around home plate, he found himself looking all the way down to the other end of the upper fields at Hayworth where the JV team was. He could see Coach Leeman in the distance going into that goofy full windup of his.

In that moment Nick couldn't believe how much he wanted to be down there catching him, wanted to be back with *his* team in the worst way.

The JV team, that was his baseball family.

Nick could tell that already.

Already he was hoping that Bobby Mazzilli was a fast healer, maybe the fastest in history.

Nick Crandall's first varsity practice never did get any better.

When it was his turn to hit, Steve Carberry strapped on the gear and went behind the plate. And when Nick, after a few weak grounders and some wild swings and misses, finally managed a weak fly ball to left-field, Steve said, "Shoot, I lost the bet."

"What bet?" Nick said.

"The one with Jack that you couldn't get the ball out of the infield."

"Sorry," Nick said.

Then as Nick was walking away, he heard this from behind him: "Quit now."

It could have been Steve, could have been somebody over near the bench on the first-base side of the field, Nick wasn't sure. When he turned around, all he saw was Steve settling into his crouch, waiting for Coach Williams to pitch to Joey Johnson.

"What?" Nick said.

Now Steve turned. "You talking to me?"

"Yeah."

Steve flipped his mask back, and when he did, Nick could see the big smile on his face. "I didn't say anything," Steve said.

By then, it didn't matter whether he had or hadn't. His message, and Gary Watson's, had already been delivered loud and clear.

When Joey had finished taking his cuts, Coach Williams told Nick to get his equipment back on while everybody took a water break.

Nick went to the end of the bench, alone, put his knee pads on first, the way he always did, then slipped his chest protector over his head. When he was finished, he saw that Coach Williams had come over to sit next to him.

"I know this has been a rough day for you," he said.

"I can't do *anything*."

"*Today,*" Coach Williams said. "You can't do anything today. You must feel like this is your first day at school all over again."

"More like I'm *getting* schooled," Nick said.

"It will get better, I promise."

"No it won't."

"Sure it will." Coach Williams gently turned Nick around a little bit on the bench, so Nick was facing him. "Look at me," he said.

Nick did.

"It's gotta work," Coach Williams said. "And I'll tell you why: Because if you look bad, so do I."

Nick said, "No, no, no, this is on me."

"Now, that's where you're *really* wrong," Coach Williams said. "Because this deal is on both of us. For however long we're together."

Nick settled down a little bit after that. He still wasn't throwing the way he knew he could, still hadn't nailed a single guy trying to steal. There was too much air underneath most of his throws, but at least he was getting them to second and third on the fly, wasn't skipping balls past his fielders or shooting them so far over their heads they would have needed brooms to knock them down.

Still, when Coach Williams announced that Conor Bell was going to be the last batter of the day, Nick was relieved. Usually he didn't want practice to end. It wasn't that he didn't want to get home, now that he had a real home. It was just that baseball, even baseball practice, was the best and most fun part of his day, and he never wanted the fun to stop.

Today he was happy that practice was finally going to be over, the way you were happy when you got dismissed from your last class in school.

There were runners on second and third, two out. Coach Williams yelled in to Conor that he better have his helmet on tight, because he planned on striking him out.

"You got nothing, Coach," Conor said.

"Even when I got nothing, I got enough to punch you out."

"Bring it," Conor said.

Everybody on the field knew that they were just having fun, that neither of them meant what they were saying as trash talk. Especially not Conor Bell. From what Nick had seen, he was one of the cooler kids on the varsity team. And he hadn't gone out of his way once to dog Nick the way Gary and Steve had.

One time when he was running off the field, he had veered a little so he could run past Nick and tell him to hang in there.

Now he dug his back foot in and said to Nick, "Watch the swing I'm going to put on this baby."

He went after the first pitch he saw, went after it with a huge swing, as promised, but the best he could do was pop the ball straight up in the air.

Nick wasn't sure whether it was going to be fair or foul. He just knew, with this sixth sense he had—catcher's radar—that it was going to land somewhere close to home plate.

Cake, he thought.

Finally.

"Mine!" he yelled, even as he could see Steve coming down from first and Gary Watson, playing third with Conor batting, racing in from the other direction.

Nick casually tossed his mask away, looked up for the ball. And right into the last of the afternoon sun.

It blinded him just for a second.

Nick stuck his catcher's mitt straight up in the air, trying to use it as a shade. Out of the corner of his eyes, he could see one runner coming hard from third, then another right behind him, just on the chance that the ball would land in fair territory.

At the last second, Nick spotted the ball. It was on its way down, just a little to the right of the plate, up the first baseline, not so far from where he had originally thought it was going to be.

His arm wasn't working today, but at least his radar was.

He kept his glove hand in the air now, just moved a couple of steps to his right.

As he did, he tripped over his mask.

Tripped over the stupid mask and stumbled backward and couldn't do anything to stop himself.

He ended up sitting down—hard—just outside the batter's box on the infield grass, facing the pitcher's mound as the ball landed squarely on top of his head.

It didn't hurt nearly as much as the laughter that seemed to come from all over the varsity field.

SIX

Of all the comic book heroes, Nick liked Captain Marvel the best.

He didn't care much for the newer version, the one that barely reminded Nick of the original, where they'd not only changed the way Captain Marvel looked, but a lot of the backstory.

He preferred the original version, because you don't mess with a story like this, about an orphan named Billy Batson, who only had to speak the name of this ancient wizard—*Shazam!*—to be "magically transformed from boy to man—the world's mightiest mortal!"

There were other comic book heroes Nick liked. He had always liked reading about the Justice League of America, which Captain Marvel would still show up to help once in a while, the way he'd show up to help out in some of the Superman comic books.

Nick also liked Batman a lot, because Bruce Wayne's parents had been killed by bad guys the way Billy Batson's had been killed by Sivana.

But as far as he was concerned, Batman on his best day couldn't touch Captain Marvel. Neither could the Fantastic Four or Aquaman or Daredevil, not just in the *real* old comic books that Mr. Boyd had first shown him, from his own collection, but much later, a more modern version, from what was called the Shazam series.

It had started accidentally enough one day in Riverdale, when Mrs. Boyd had stopped to pick up soft drinks at a convenience store in a mall not far from where they lived. Next door to it was a store called Cards and Collectibles, where you could buy old baseball cards and signed pictures of old players and even rare coins. Nick asked if they could stop in there for a second, just to look around. While they were in there, he found himself in front of a display of antique comic books.

It was there that he found a copy of one of the oldest Captain Marvels. And because the cover was torn and a couple of pages were ready to fall right out, the store had discounted the price.

He had asked Mrs. Boyd if she would buy it for him. She said sure. When she saw what it was, Nick remembered how she smiled at him.

"Young man, you're gonna make an old man real happy today," she'd said.

"Why?" Nick had asked, and she'd said Nick would find out when he got home.

Later that evening, Mr. Boyd showed Nick what he called his "secret stash" of old comic books, in a box he kept in the closet of his bedroom. It turned out he still had a few of the original Captain Marvels, back from the 1940s. Mr. Boyd said they were worth good money now to collectors.

Then he added that it didn't make any difference to him, because his weren't for sale.

"I used to collect these the way other people collect stamps or baseball cards," he said.

Nick fell in love with Captain Marvel that day, with Billy Batson, the orphan kid who, when he wasn't turning himself into Captain Marvel, was a reporter for what was known as WHIZ radio.

"Probably be sports-talk radio, all these people yelling at each other, now," Mr. Boyd had said.

There were so many things Nick loved about Captain Marvel, and one of them was the way he'd made a family for himself over the years. He had a sister, Mary Bromfield, who had a different name from Billy because she'd been adopted by a different family. And he had an Uncle Marvel in some of the comics. And there was even a Junior Captain Marvel, a boy named Freddy who'd gotten hurt one time in a fierce battle between Captain Marvel and a guy called Captain Nazi.

To make up for Freddy getting hurt, Captain Marvel had given some of his powers to him, and so later Freddy only had to say "Captain Marvel"—not *Shazam!*—to turn himself into a junior crimefighter.

Maybe that was the part Nick loved the best, that all you had to do to make things come out the way you wanted them to was say a magic word.

Then you were ready to slug it out with Sivana or Mister Mind or Black Adam.

Or Gary Watson or Steve Carberry.

If only, Nick thought.

When he'd left the Boyds to come live with the Crandalls, Mr. Boyd had let him keep all the Captain Marvels from that box of his and presented him with the last of the Shazam series from the 1970s that he'd been buying up for Nick online and giving him as presents from time to time. By the time Nick went to live with the Crandalls, he had all thirty-five comic books in the Shazam series.

"Someday you can pass them along to a boy of your own," Mr. Boyd had said. "'Less you sell them for big bucks first."

"I'll never sell them," Nick had said the night he was packing them up. "They're the most valuable thing I've ever owned in my life."

So by now he knew just about everything about Captain Marvel, *all* the versions of him, reading up on him on the Internet the way he would his favorite ballplayers. He didn't like comics as much as he liked baseball—you couldn't *play* comics after all, not even the way most guys his age liked to play video games—but they came in a close second.

His favorite Captain Marvel stories of all were the ones where Billy was guided by the spirit of his real dad, C. C. Batson, who'd show up occasionally, even if Billy never knew when it was going to happen.

One day Nick was telling Gracie about those stories, telling her how cool he thought it was that Billy Batson finally got to know his real dad, even if it was just in the form of a ghost.

Gracie just looked at him and said, "You've got a real dad now, Captain."

Tonight, though, Nick didn't want to be anywhere near his dad, not the one telling him to get upstairs and do his homework. Nick needed Captain Marvel tonight, so he was on his bed with the door closed, reading one of the first comic books he'd ever read, about this huge beatdown between the Captain and Black Adam, the bad guy who pretty much had equal powers, even if the Captain always found a way to win in the end.

Most nights, Nick wanted to watch baseball if he finished his homework on time. Tonight, though, he didn't want to even think about it, not after the way practice had gone, not with the goose egg he still had on his head where the ball had clipped him on the way down. This was one of those times when he wished he had a baseball dad, one who didn't just know the game but had played it at Nick's age, who knew what it was like to have the kind of day he'd had at practice. And what did Paul Crandall know about failing or coming up short, anyway? He was the smartest person Nick had ever been around.

What could he possibly understand about being the kind of total loser Nick had been out on that field?

Maybe tomorrow he could get his baseball powers back. But tonight, he needed to get lost in his comics.

Nick knew he was supposed to be doing homework. He had promised his English professor dad and his math professor mom that he was going straight upstairs after dessert to crack open his schoolbooks.

He went with comic books instead.

And became so lost in Captain Marvel's world that he didn't hear his dad's footsteps on the stairs or hear the door open or even know he was standing there in the doorway until he heard his voice.

"For which class would that book be?"

Busted.

"I just didn't feel much like studying tonight," he said.

"But you told us downstairs you were coming up here to work," Paul Crandall said.

"And I meant to," Nick said. "But when I got up here, I changed my mind."

"Well, you need to unchange it, young man. Unless you're under the impression that your grades are just going to magically improve on their own. As if they're the ones with the magic powers."

"Maybe they're not going to improve this year no matter what I do."

"Nick, there's no way of knowing that unless you try. And one way to do that is to get your nose out of those comic books of yours once in a while."

"But I like comic books better than real books!" he said, just blurting it out, realizing as soon as he did that real books were pretty much his dad's whole life.

Nick was afraid for a second he might have made everything worse. But his dad just said, "Maybe if you gave real books a chance, you'd find out that they have heroes just like your Captain Marvel."

"Like who?" Nick said.

"Well, when I was a boy," his dad said, "my absolute favorite books were the ones about King Arthur and Lancelot and the Knights of the Round Table."

"That's the one about the sword in the stone, right?" Nick said.

He could see the excitement on Paul Crandall's face. "You know it?"

"My friend Jack says it was his favorite cartoon movie when he was little."

"You never watched it?"

"No," Nick said, wishing in that moment that he had.

Paul Crandall smiled to himself, nodding. "Anyway . . . Lancelot was my favorite," he said. "And I was thinking you might find him to be kind of . . . cool. Because even though his parents were royalty— the king and queen of Benwick—he was raised by somebody else, the Lady of the Lake."

"Sort of like an orphan," Nick said.

"Sort of."

"Did he go up against any bad guys?"

"The baddest, as you and your friends might

say," Paul Crandall said. "Sir Turquine. He turned evil and imprisoned over sixty of King Arthur's knights." He was smiling broadly now. "And he did *very* well when he had to go up against giants. And I don't mean the San Francisco Giants." He was still smiling as he said, "The stories about those knights are as good as there are in the history of stories. You should read them sometime."

"Maybe I will," Nick said, knowing there was *no* chance of that happening anytime soon. He was far enough behind with the books he was supposed to be reading.

There was a silence between them then, a big one, as if neither one knew how to end this. Finally Paul Crandall said, "Nick, you were awfully quiet at dinner tonight."

"I'm fine," he said.

Nick knew that what had happened at practice was probably something a boy was supposed to talk about with his dad. But he wasn't in the mood. He hadn't even wanted to talk about baseball with Gracie tonight.

If his dad didn't get it with comic books, which

were at least books, even if they did have cool pictures in them, how was he possibly going to understand what had happened on that field today?

"You're sure."

"Yeah," Nick said. Then: "I'll do my homework now. Promise this time."

Paul Crandall said he'd look in on Nick when it was time to say good night, then closed the door behind him. Nick went over and sat down at his desk and opened his math book to where his assignment page was.

In that moment he couldn't decide what he wanted more, for his math problems to disappear or his baseball problems.

Without even realizing he was doing it, Nick brought his hand to the bump on the top of his head.

Shazam, Nick thought.

Shazam, shazam, shazam.

SEVEN

Usually during free period Nick would play Wiffle ball. Because once they got to spring at Hayworth and the weather started to get nice and turn into baseball weather, Wiffle ball was about the biggest thing going with seventh-grade boys.

They'd go down to the huge lawn by the new upper-school building, called the Randolph building, and every day was like a brand-new World Series of Wiffle. The teams changed every day, but the fun of being out here, playing ball for an hour during school, trying as hard as you could to hit a home run every time up, to hit one farther than anybody else that day, never changed.

One time, in the middle of a game, Ollie Brown looked at Nick and said, "This is more fun than fun."

If you asked the guys playing what their favorite class was at Hayworth, Nick knew just about every one of them would say the same thing: Wiffle.

On their way out of English class today, during which Nick had been called out by Mr. Dodds for not having done his required reading the night before, Nick announced to Zach and Ollie and Jeff, all of whom were in Mr. Dodds's class with him, that he was skipping Wiffle just this once.

"What's the matter, you're too cool for us now that you're on *varsity*?" Zach said.

Nick didn't really think Zach was serious. As far as they could tell, Zach was never too serious about anything, except maybe the Boston Red Sox. He was still taking a little bit of a shot, though.

Nick thought, If he thinks *I* think I'm cool because of varsity, he has *no* clue, zero and zip, about what happened yesterday.

"You've got enough guys," Nick said. "There's always enough guys."

"C'mon, dude," Ollie said. "Now that you're a big star on varsity, Wiffle is the only ballin' we're gonna get to do with you."

Jeff Kantor grinned. "You can tell us what it's like to make the Show."

Jeff put air quotes with his fingers around "the Show." They were all huge baseball fans; it was the main reason they hung around together, and so they all knew the Show was another way of saying the big leagues.

Nick wondered how he could get it from both directions now, his new varsity teammates and his old JV teammates.

The only difference was, he knew these guys actually cared what happened to him, unlike the guys who were supposed to be his teammates now.

"No kidding," Nick said. "*Horror* show is more like it. The way I played yesterday with those guys, we're probably gonna be together again real soon, and not just on the Wiffle ball field."

They all tried to change his mind one more time. When they realized it wasn't going to happen, that Nick was really going to take a day off, they ran down toward the lawn next to Randolph and Nick walked by himself toward the smaller lawn in the middle of the circular driveway in front of the main administration building. That was where the kids who just wanted to chill went to hang out during free period if it was a nice day, like today.

That's where he found Gracie.

She was sitting alone on a bench reading. Not a schoolbook. Just the latest book she was reading for fun, one with a funny picture of a fish on the front, with a toilet seat around his neck, called *Flush*. No surprise there. Gracie was always reading. Sometimes they'd be either in her mom's car or Mrs. Crandall's car for a ride across town, and Gracie would whip out a book in the backseat and start reading if Nick was listening to a ballgame on the radio.

"Hey," Nick said.

She looked up, immediately marked her page and closed the book. Smiled at him. "Hey, Captain," she said.

Then right away she said, "Are you sick?"

"No," Nick said. "Why'd you ask me that?"

"I just figured you had to be sick if you're not down there with your boys trying to be the Wiffle king of Hayworth."

Nick sat down next to her. "I'd probably stink at that, too," he said, then told her as fast as he could about everything that had happened at practice.

"I was wondering why you didn't call last night or instant message me," she said.

"I didn't feel like talking about it," he said. "Or typing about it."

"I already knew, anyway," Gracie said.

"How?"

"Jack told me last night. *He* IM-ed me."

"Well, I hope he didn't tell the whole school," Nick said.

He had been with Gracie when she was IM-ing people. Sometimes it would look as if she had about six conversations going at once. Nick would get worn out just watching her—it was like she was using her keyboard the way a juggler would.

"Just me," Gracie said. "And you know I don't talk, no matter what."

Nick leaned his head back as far as he could, staring straight into the sun the way he had trying to catch that foul ball.

"I gotta find a way to get out of this," he said.

"Well, at least you've got a good attitude about everything," Gracie said, giving him one of her elbows to the ribs.

"Is that supposed to be sarcastic?"

As if he didn't know.

"It's not supposed to be anything except me telling you to stop acting like a baby," Gracie said. "You have one bad day and you're ready to quit?"

"What I'm not ready for is varsity."

"Stop being such a whiner," she said. "I mean it. You know how much I hate it when you turn into a mopey mope."

Nick still had his head back, remembering how practice had ended. "You didn't hear the way they all laughed when I got plunked right on top of my head."

Gracie said, "You have to admit, if it had happened to somebody else, you would have thought it was pretty funny, too."

"Thanks. But you wouldn't think everything was so funny if you heard some of the little comments they made when they thought the coach couldn't hear."

"Boo hoo," Gracie Wright said.

"You weren't there, is all I'm saying."

"Wouldn't have made any difference if I had been," she said. "Because I know something they don't know on the dopey varsity."

"What?"

"You're tougher than they are."

"Yeah, right."

"I *am* right. The only problem sometimes is that you don't know how tough you are."

Before Nick could come up with an answer for that, he heard a cheer from down the hill, sat up straight and looked down there and saw Ollie circling the bases, saw Zach retrieving the ball past the tree line at the end of the lawn, which in their game meant only one thing:

Home run.

"At least somebody's having fun at baseball today," Nick said.

"You can, too," Gracie said. "It's like something my mom says when she's telling me I can do something I don't think I can."

As if that ever happened, Nick thought. She thought she could do anything except fly.

And maybe even that.

Gracie said, "My mom just tells me to get out of my own way."

"I couldn't even get out of my own way trying to catch one ridonkulously easy foul pop," Nick said.

"So today will be better," Gracie said, and said it so convincingly that she almost started to convince Nick.

Today there was no team meeting before the start of practice, which was just fine with Nick, since he didn't feel like part of this team any more than he had the day before.

They did some stretching drills first, Coach Williams saying they were going to start doing them every day, that you were never too young to stretch before sports. Then he announced it was going to be a very busy day for the Hayworth Tigers, infield first and then batting practice and then baserunning and then some scrimmaging, if they had time.

"We've only got ten games in our season," Coach Williams said. "And as most of you probably know, there's no play-offs in our league, for the simple reason that we don't have enough time to get them in before the end of the school year.

"Anyway," he continued, "our first game is next Tuesday, so we've all got to think of our first week of practice as being like the last week of spring training for teams in the majors. Which means we've got a lot of work to do in a real short amount of time."

Tell me about it, Nick thought.

"One more thing," Coach Williams said. "Everybody who goes to this school knows that we've only got one huge rival, and that's King. Who has beaten us the last five years running. In addition to them going undefeated the last three. This year they're our fourth game, so circle that date on your calendar. And, gentlemen? We are going to be ready."

Early in practice there wasn't a lot for Nick to do. While Coach hit grounders to the infielders, Nick just stood next to him, catching the ball when the guys lobbed it back in.

Even doing something as simple as that, he felt everybody watching him, same as yesterday.

It made him remember the first day he'd played T-ball in Riverdale, way before that day at Shea Stadium had turned baseball into something he lived and breathed. They were called the Riverdale

Redbirds, even had the bird that looked like the St. Louis Cardinals bird on the front of their red caps.

Nick didn't remember the caps as well as the feeling he had when he got to the field and looked around and realized there wasn't a single kid on the field he knew.

That day, standing at the edge of the parking lot right behind the backstop, holding on as hard as he could to Mr. Boyd's hand, he'd said, "I want to go home now, please."

They had gotten there late, so all the other kids had their red caps and red T-shirts already, and were lined up getting ready to swing away at the ball on the tee.

"C'mon," Mr. Boyd had said, half walking Nick and half tugging him toward the field. "You don't know it today, but someday fields like this are gonna feel like home to you."

"I don't know anybody," Nick had said, still holding on to his hand.

"Those boys out there, they're the same as you. All they care about is hitting that little ball."

Afterward, long afterward, one night when Mr. Boyd and Nick were watching a Mets game on television, they were talking about that first day and Mr. Boyd had said, "We did the right thing. If we'd gone home that day, you might never have gone back."

"I was just a little afraid."

And Mr. Boyd had said, "Everybody's afraid of something in sports. Of failing, mostly. The best ones are just best at getting past it."

I have to find a way to do that now, Nick thought. Today.

Even though there was a part of him that felt like a Riverdale Redbird again, wanting to leave this field and go straight home.

In batting practice, Nick was at least hitting the ball today, getting some good line drives off the coach—one to left, one to center, one to right.

"Way to use the whole ballpark there, Nick!" Coach Williams said.

Nick thought, He makes it sound like I just won the game with a grand-slam home run.

"See?" Jack Elmore said when Nick's turn at bat was over and Jack's was about to start. "I *knew* you'd remember which end of the bat you're supposed to use!"

Nick said, "Just so you know? You're not helping, as funny as you think you are."

Jack grinned. "Dude. I'm not good enough to help."

They both knew it was true. Maybe if his best friend on his team was also the best player on the team, he could have helped out with the other guys. But Jack wasn't close to being the best player, which meant that Nick was pretty much on his own with the other guys. None of whom had said anything to him today. Nick couldn't decide which was worse, the kind of stuff he'd heard from Gary yesterday, or the silent treatment he was getting now.

Either way, he was still an outsider.

Nick was good at that by now.

When the team got around to scrimmaging, he went back to feeling as if he'd forgotten how to play. It was as if his equipment, even his red-and-yellow mask that he'd painted in Captain Marvel colors, was on backward. As if his throwing arm still wouldn't work right. He'd hear baseball announcers saying sometimes that pitchers who couldn't throw a strike to save their lives had "lost" the strike zone, the way you lost a pen or a notebook in school.

Nick felt as if he had lost more than the strike zone. He never came close to throwing out any of the guys trying to steal a base on him.

Every throw was different. Bounce one. Sail one. Throw one wide. If I keep this up, Nick thought, I'm gonna end up like one of those pitchers who get so wild they have to finally switch positions.

After the first six guys had stolen on him, Coach Williams called time and started walking toward home plate. On the previous pitch, Nick had air-mailed one into center field, even though the runner trying to get to second was Steve Carberry, the slowest guy on the team.

Gary Watson was the batter. As Nick stood there and helplessly watched the ball go so far over Joey Johnson's head he didn't even bother to jump for it, Gary was finally ready to say something.

"Dude," he said in a loud voice, "are you absolutely sure you're right-handed?"

Coach Williams said, "Gary," and made a motion with his hand for Gary to walk away from the plate for a second.

To Nick he quietly said, "You've got to find a way to relax."

"I *can't*," Nick said.

"Nick, this is baseball, not life and death."

Nick wanted to tell him he was wrong, it was *much* more important than that to him. Or at least it felt that way right now.

Nick had taken off his Captain Marvel mask, had it in his hand, his cap turned around backward on his head, the way catchers did. And just like that, he could feel his eyes start to fill up with tears.

He tried to look away. But Coach Williams saw. Grown-ups could always see tears coming, even from a mile away.

Crying in front of the whole team would be all I need, he thought, squeezing his eyes shut like he was thinking real hard about what the coach was saying to him.

Then he quickly put his mask back on.

Needing the mask in that moment as much as he ever had.

"You know what?" Coach Williams said. "I just had a brilliant thought."

He yelled, "Listen up!" and told everybody that Gary would be the last batter of the day—they were going to quit a little early. Then he jogged back to the mound, Gary hit a liner to Joey Johnson and Coach said it had been a great practice, for everybody to pick up and he'd see them tomorrow.

As the rest of the guys started to leave, Nick sat at the end of the bench on the first-base side and started to take off his gear.

Coach came over and said, "Leave it on for a second."

"How come?"

"Just leave it on."

Joey Johnson was the last of the varsity players to leave the bench area. When he did, catching up with everybody else as they walked toward the gym, Coach Williams said, "Okay, then."

This must be when he tells me he's sending me back to JV.

The thought of *that* didn't make Nick want to cry; it made him feel relieved more than anything.

"It really is okay, Coach," Nick said. Trying to help him break the news.

If Coach Williams had heard what Nick said, he didn't let on, just stood up and said, "Let's get to work."

"Work?"

Nick felt a little bit like he was getting kept after class for doing something wrong. In this case, it just happened to be baseball class.

"Well, work in the sense that we have to work to get you to start playing baseball again," Coach Williams said. "Make you feel the way you did when you first started playing ball."

Nick said he didn't understand.

Coach Williams said he'd show him.

For the next half hour, just the two of them on the varsity field, that is *exactly* what he did.

They played.

It was like he was a Riverdale Redbird all over again.

EIGHT

The first thing Coach Williams did was take out his car keys.

Took them out, handed them to Nick at home plate, walked away until he was halfway between Nick and the pitcher's mound, turned around with this great big grin on his face, as if he knew something that Nick didn't.

"Toss me the keys," Coach Williams said.

"Toss you the keys?"

"Yes, sir."

"Can I ask why?"

"No."

"Okaaay."

"No questions, no comments. Just throw me the keys."

Nick tossed him the keys, underhanded.

Coach caught them and tossed them back.

"Again."

Nick didn't say anything this time, just threw back the keys.

"Good," Coach said, and then came back to where Nick was standing.

"What just happened here?" he said to Nick. "Oh, wait. I know. You made two perfect throws. If I hadn't grabbed the suckers with my hand, they would have hit me in the middle of the chest both times."

"I threw you your keys," Nick said, "not a baseball."

"I don't care if you were throwing me a bag of peanuts like those vendors do at the ballpark," Coach Williams said. "The point is, you didn't *think* about making a perfect throw. You didn't worry about putting too much on the ball. Or whether you were throwing sidearm or coming over the top. You didn't worry, period. I said throw, you threw."

Nick said, "It's not that easy when it's for real."

"With an arm like you've got?" Coach said. "Yeah, it is. Or at least it should be."

"I feel like I've got to make a perfect throw every time to show these guys I belong."

"You're *kidding*!" Coach Williams said. Acting shocked in a funny way. "I hadn't picked up on that at *all*."

"I know what you're trying to do," Nick said. "It's just that the harder I try—"

"The worse you throw. And even worse than that, the worse you think you look."

Nick decided to just come right out with it, before he wasted any more of Coach Williams's time.

Get this over with once and for all.

"You should find another catcher now, before the season starts," he said. "And send me back to JV where I belong."

"No," he said. He clapped his hands together, as if the fun were really about to start now. "Now that we've conquered key throwing, let's advance to baseball throwing."

Coach Williams went over to the old canvas ball bag and began rolling balls in front of the plate. Maybe ten or twelve of them. When he was done, he lined them neatly up in the dirt, at the edge of the batter's box closest to the pitcher's mound.

Then he grabbed his glove out of the bag and jogged out to second base.

"Drill's simple enough," he said to Nick. "Start on either side. Pick up the ball on the end and throw the sucker. Then the next one. And the next. There's only one rule: no hesitation between throws. Imagine it's like that three-point shooting contest they have at the NBA All-Star game and I've got the clock on. You've got just long enough to pick out your target—that would be me—and let those babies fly."

"One question," Nick said.

"Shoot."

"Can I wear my mask?"

"Knock yourself out. Then start trying to knock *me* over with that arm of yours."

Nick fixed his mask in place as if this were a real game and he was getting ready for the next batter and the next pitch. The mask really was a beauty, what Paul and Brenda had called his Opening Day present, even though they actually gave it to him as a surprise a few days before JV practice had started.

"So technically it's Opening Day because you're

opening it now," Brenda Crandall had said, and Nick could see how pleased she was that she'd made a little joke, then even more pleased at how excited Nick had been, in a Christmas way, when he'd opened the box sitting there that morning on the table in the kitchen.

It was exactly the one he'd wanted, the one he'd been checking out on the Internet, the Rawlings Coolflo hockey-style catcher's mask, the Pro 2.

Today, more than ever, Nick needed it to be his superhero mask.

He needed to get his powers back, at least to show this coach, the one who kept saying he believed in him so much, that he did have some game after all.

Right now he didn't care about Gary Watson and the other guys.

Just this coach.

"Go!" Coach Williams yelled.

Nick picked up the first ball in the line and promptly sailed it over coach's head.

But before he could hang his head for long, just at the idea that this one-on-one practice was starting out exactly the way real practice had ended, he heard Coach Williams say, "You're on the clock, dude. Throw the keys."

Nick picked up the next ball and let it rip. It wasn't perfect, but it had some steam on it, and Coach Williams managed to grab it without taking his foot off the bag. Even made a sweep tag on an imaginary runner for show.

On the third ball, Nick fired a strike.

Then another one.

And another.

By the last couple of balls, he wasn't even looking where he threw. He could picture Coach standing there, feet straddling the bag.

Better yet, he felt like he knew exactly where the ball was going.

He was sweating when they finished, and out of breath. The good kind of tired you could get in sport. But the only rest he got was when Coach Williams jogged back in from second to put the balls back in the line in the dirt in front of the plate.

"Again," he said.

When he had gotten halfway through the second group and was five-for-five throwing strikes down to second, Coach Williams told him he could stop. Nick's arm was tired—not that he was going to admit that in about ten thousand years—but he didn't care. When he tipped the mask back off his face, he couldn't help it. He was smiling.

On the varsity field.

Coach Williams tossed his own glove away as he passed the pitcher's mound, smiling himself. "If you can do it with me here today, you can do it with your teammates tomorrow."

"Can I tell you something, Coach?"

"You can tell me anything, son. That's going to be our deal."

"They don't feel much like my teammates."

"They will," Coach Williams said.

"How do you know?"

"Because they're gonna start seeing what I see in you."

"What's that?"

"A guy born to be a catcher," Coach said. "It's in your blood, Nick. I'll bet your father was a catcher, am I right?"

For a second Nick felt the way you do when you

get hit in the stomach playing sports and get the wind knocked out of you.

The only thing he could think to do was flip the mask back down.

"No," he said in a small voice.

"I just thought, because you look like such a natural to me."

Nick didn't want to tell his coach he had no idea if his real dad had been a catcher, didn't know anything about his real dad at all.

He wasn't going to tell Coach Williams that he was adopted. He tried to figure how Gracie would get out of this, and he knew she'd try to find a way to joke her way out, but Nick didn't feel too funny right at that moment.

"No," Nick said again, "I learned how to make crummy throws all by myself."

Coach Williams rapped on the side of Nick's mask and said, "Hello, in there? Talk like that ends today."

They walked off the field together, Nick with the ball bag slung over his shoulder. Feeling all right about himself. Not great. Just all right, for a change. Because the day had ended a lot better than it began.

Like he'd come from behind a little bit in a game in which he'd been way, way behind. Not coming all the way back and winning.

Just getting back into it.

It turned out they hadn't finished much later than a normal practice would have. That was why when they came around the corner of the main administration building, Nick could see a lot of his teammates still waiting to be picked up.

Gary Watson and Steve Carberry among them. Just standing there.

Watching Nick.

Nick put his head down, started to jog toward the locker room.

It was then that he heard the jangling of some keys.

At first he thought Coach Williams had appeared out of nowhere to give him one last reminder about just reacting and throwing and not thinking so much, everything they'd spent the last half hour talking about.

But then he looked up and saw Gary Watson grinning at him, holding up a set of keys. Tossing them in the air and catching them.

They were watching, Nick thought. They hung around to watch Coach and me.

Nick stood there, unable to turn away as Gary motioned Steve to move a few feet away. Then he made a show of gently tossing Steve the keys, the way you'd toss a ball to a little baby.

NINE

The keys didn't help for long.

By the next day, Nick was back to pushing the ball toward second and third, when guys began stealing on him all over again.

He wasn't as wild as he'd been the first couple of days of practice, wasn't bouncing as many or sending as many throws to the outfield. But as soon as he was back on the field with his teammates, it was as if he got scared of his arm all over again. Before long, he was taking way too much time to release the ball and had given up on trying to use all his arm, throw with everything he had the way he used to. He just wanted to make sure to at least hit the glove he was aiming at.

He *was* throwing like a baby, pretty much.

Over the last three practices before they got to

the weekend, Coach Williams kept trying to give him pep talks, tell him he could see improvement, and every once in a while, when the rest of the Tigers weren't watching, he'd jangle those keys in his pocket.

Both Nick and his coach knew better.

They knew Nick wasn't nearly the catcher this coach had thought he was getting, and he wasn't nearly ready for his first varsity baseball game the following Tuesday.

The first Captain Marvel comic book Nick ever read explained that the magic word *Shazam* came from the first letters of Solomon, Hercules, Atlas, Zeus, Achilles and Mercury. Billy Batson, when he turned into Captain Marvel, was supposed to have gotten wisdom from Solomon, strength from Hercules, stamina from Atlas, power from Zeus, courage from Achilles and speed from Mercury.

Nick was coming up short in all those areas right now. Especially courage and speed. Even if it was only arm speed.

The weird thing was, he was starting to hit a little better, getting at least one solid hit a day. On

Friday, Nick's last time up, he had doubled off Gary Watson, the best knock he'd gotten yet, driving home a couple of runs and making it into second base standing up.

The hit seemed to make Gary Watson even more annoyed with Nick than usual.

The next guy up against him was Joey Johnson. And even though Nick wasn't taking any kind of lead, Gary wheeled before his first pitch to Joey and tried to pick Nick off. Nick dove back to the bag, because the last thing he was going to let happen after his first big hit as a varsity player—even if it was only in practice—was to get himself picked off second base because he'd let Jack Elmore sneak in behind him.

Gary's throw hit him right in the back.

Hard.

Nick was sure he'd done it on purpose. Gary hadn't tried to pick anybody off second all day, and he wasn't that wild. In the big leagues, you knew when a pitcher wanted to hit a batter. Nick was sure this was just as intentional, even if Gary was throwing toward second instead of to the plate.

"Sorry, dude," Gary said, mostly for the benefit of his teammates and Coach Williams.

"No problem," Nick said, dusting dirt off the front of his shirt.

The ball had hurt him. But no way he was going to show Gary that. It was part of what the announcers called the code of the game that you weren't supposed to rub after you got hit by the ball, no matter what.

Jack Elmore was still standing next to second when Gary turned back toward home plate.

He leaned in toward Nick, like he was still trying to keep him close. "Know why he hit you where he did?" Jack said.

"Why?"

Jack gave him a quick slap on the side of his leg with his glove. "'Cause he thought it would be too obvious trying to bounce one off your helmet, that's why."

Practice ended ten minutes later. Nick had somehow managed to survive the week. The only good thing that had happened was that double off Gary Watson. And even that turned out to be painful.

Only Jack had made any real effort to make him feel welcome. Some of the other guys would talk to him occasionally during practice, and Joey had yelled "nice hit!" after the double. Nick wasn't sure if he meant it, if any of them meant it, or if they were just doing it for show in front of the coach, now that they were stuck with him as catcher.

At least he hadn't quit. Sometimes, not too often, but sometimes, he actually thought Gracie might be right, that he was tougher than he thought he was.

Tough didn't mean he was ready for varsity ball, though.

When Nick added it all up—as bad as he usually was at math—nothing much had changed from the first day he'd practiced with the varsity.

Nobody wanted him there.

"Is it just because I'm a seventh-grader?" Nick was saying to Jack Elmore now. "Is that why these guys act as if they're going to, like, catch something from the new catcher?"

Nick and Jack and Gracie were at school on Saturday afternoon for the annual Hayworth School carnival, known as the Frogtown Fair. It was a funny name for a carnival, but Hayworth was on Frogtown Road. It wasn't the biggest or best carnival in the world, not like the one they'd have outside of town during the summer. But there were a lot of games, and contests, and cool prizes, and even a Ferris wheel that the fire department had set up for them.

Pretty much the whole school turned out for it, especially when the weather was as perfect as it was today.

For Nick it was a chance to hang with his two best friends and not think about baseball for a change.

Except he had just asked Jack this one question, like he'd dropped his guard for a second.

He just wanted to understand why guys who were supposed to be his teammates were making this so much harder for him than it already was.

"You want the truth?" Jack said.

"He can't handle the truth!" Gracie yelled.

They both looked at her as if she'd just stuck her ice cream cone in her ear.

She shook her head, this sad, sad look on her face. "It's from a famous movie," she said.

Jack said to Nick, "*Do* you want the truth?"

"Yeah."

"Just give it to him in little sips," Gracie said, taking a big lick of chocolate ice cream, leaving marks all around her mouth. "Like when you have to take yucky cough medicine."

"Wellllll," Jack said, "some of the guys—not all, just some—think you're too small to play catcher. That's one thing."

"But I'm not even close to being small for my age," Nick said in protest.

"For your age," Jack said. "But remember, we're talking about varsity."

"Boys," Gracie said to herself, shaking her head again. She did that a lot when she was hanging around with them. "You ever hear girls talking about varsity like it's one of those secret societies in Nick's comics?"

"I'm just saying," Jack said. He paused and said, "And it's more than that, and more than Coach Williams treating you like teacher's pet."

"That's not my fault, that he's trying to make me stink less."

"I'm not saying it is," Jack said. "You're the one who asked."

"What else?" Nick said.

Jack took a deep breath and let it out and finally said, "They *do* think you stink. Mostly at throwing."

"But throwing is his best thing!" Gracie said.

"Not this week," Nick said.

"You don't forget how to throw in a week, Captain," she said.

"See, the thing is, Bobby Mazzilli was *great* at throwing people out," Jack said. "He didn't have the kind of arm you do, but he had this quick release, and it made his arm seem stronger than it really was. Not only did he save a bunch of games for us last year, by the end of the year, guys were afraid to run on him." Jack gave Nick a serious look, no jokes now, and said, "They think guys are gonna run wild on you. Just like we did all week in practice."

"They're right," Nick said.

"You don't know that," Gracie said. "You haven't even played a game yet."

"If you can't do it in practice," Nick said, "why would anybody think you can do it in a game?"

"This is the dumbest conversation I've ever had with you guys," Gracie said, "and I'm not really even in it."

Then she smiled and said, "Come on. You're about to prove you can still throw. At the dunking booth."

When they got there it was almost a dream situation for Nick. His English teacher, Mr. Dodds, had just begun his turn in the Easy Dunker.

Mr. Dodds was on the side of the dunker to Nick's left, sitting behind a screen like the one behind the plate in baseball, which protected him from getting hit by the balls, if not from the small pool of water underneath him.

Next to Mr. Dodds was the target, a white bull's-eye with a black circle around it, set in the middle of a bright yellow wall.

Nick knew other teachers had taken turns in the

booth, and not just seventh-grade teachers. When they'd first shown up at the fair, Hayworth's headmaster, Mr. Garson, had been in the hot seat, drawing the longest line of the day.

Now it was Mr. Dodds, who seemed to be smiling and having a good time—the opposite of the way he was in class, where he hardly ever cracked a smile. Where he was most famous for what was known as the Stare.

"Now, that is what I call a sitting duck," Gracie said.

Nick said, "But if I put him in the water, he'll probably dog me more than he already does."

"Dude," Jack said, "how many times are you going to have this kind of clear shot at him?"

"One of you guys do it," Nick said. "The way I'm going, I'll probably bust one of the kindergarten windows."

Gracie took Nick by the arm, putting him third in the line, telling him he didn't even have to use his own tickets to pay for his throws, he could use hers.

"Thanks so much," Nick said.

It was when he'd moved up to second in the

line—the first kid had missed all three times, so Mr. Dodds was still dry for now—that Nick saw the group of varsity baseball players walking around the corner of the lower school building.

Please, Nick thought. Please don't let them see me standing here, like I'm in the on-deck circle.

The last thing he needed was an audience, even for something as simple as trying to dunk his English teacher.

This really wasn't supposed to be about baseball today. Today was supposed to be all silly stuff at the Frogtown Fair. All week long in baseball, every single practice, Nick had felt everybody watching him. And he'd stunk.

It was why he'd promised himself he wasn't going to pick up a ball all weekend long. Just take a little break until Monday, then pretend he was starting over again, the day before their opener against Valley Falls.

That was his plan for the weekend: Come to the fair, hang with Gracie and Jack, then read comics.

Maybe even do a little of Mr. Dodds's homework.

Only now here came his baseball season right

around the corner and right at him. Gary Watson. Steve Carberry. Joey Johnson. John Fox, the second-best pitcher on varsity after Gary. All of them with ice cream cones in their hands.

"Wow, here comes your very own cheering section," Jack said.

"*Booing* section is more like it," Nick said.

When the varsity players got close, Nick could hear Gary Watson say, "Hey, look who's up! Our new backstop."

Steve Carberry said, "Mr. Dodds has nothing to worry about. He's not going anywhere near the water with Crandall throwing."

They all laughed. And it was clear that they weren't going anywhere until Nick made the three throws that Gracie had already paid for.

"Oh, just ignore them," Gracie said.

Nick wanted to tell them it would be easier to ignore a fastball somebody had thrown right up in his grill, but he didn't, he just tried to pretend as if Gary and the rest of them weren't even there.

"C'mon, Crandall!" Mr. Dodds yelled from the Easy Dunker, trying to give him the Stare. "You know you want to dunk me the way you would a basketball."

"Yeah," Gary Watson chimed in. "Let's see that famous arm of yours we keep hearing so much about."

Nick gave a quick look in Gary's direction—he couldn't help himself—and noticed a few more of his teammates had suddenly appeared.

What, he thought, did they make some kind of announcement all over the grounds?

Step right up and watch Nick Crandall, the rag-armed catcher, try to sink an English teacher?

"Just put the first one on the target and let's get out of here," Gracie said.

"Right," Nick said.

One more time he wanted to be as brave as Gracie Wright.

Or just *be* Gracie.

"Come on, it's barely more than a throw back to the pitcher," Jack said into Nick's ear. "Cake."

Mrs. Carey, the seventh-grade science teacher, had handed Gracie the balls, old scuffed-up base-balls. Gracie gave one to Nick.

"Only one you're going to need, Captain," she said.

Off to the side Nick heard Gary Watson, trying to sound like a public address announcer at the ballpark, say in a deep voice, "Now pitching for the Hayworth Tigers, their *catcher,* young Nick Crandall."

Now the other varsity players with him started chanting his name.

Nick, Nick, Nick.

Clapping as they did, having a good old time.

Nick felt himself squeezing the dirty baseball in his right hand, like he was trying to squeeze the seams right off the sucker.

Let it go, he told himself.

Throw the stupid ball.

Only he couldn't do it. Couldn't raise his arm. Couldn't make this one stupid throw.

Just stood there with the ball, arm hanging at his side.

"I can't do this," he said, handed the ball back to Gracie. Walked away.

He wasn't even going to look back, not even

when the hoots from behind him seemed to be chasing him as he moved toward the varsity field.

But then he heard the splash and the huge cheer that followed.

Nick couldn't help himself. He turned around and saw that Gracie had hit the target and put Mr. Dodds in the water.

TEN

"What the heck happened back there?" Gracie said when she finally caught up with him near the Frogtown Road entrance to the school, where her mom was supposed to pick them up.

"You saw what happened," Nick said. "I froze."

"I get that part," Gracie said, lowering her voice even though there was no one else around. "What I don't get is why."

"I was *afraid*," Nick said. "Afraid I couldn't even make a dumb little throw like that."

Gracie wasn't about to drop it. "Because the other guys on the team showed up?"

Nick said he didn't want to talk about it anymore. And he didn't, just stood there in silence with Gracie, waiting for her mom to pick them up. He knew how hard it was for Gracie not to talk about something when she really wanted to, or when she wanted to fix things for Nick. But even she was quiet now, and on the ride home.

When they were both out of the car and Nick was walking down the Wrights' driveway, all she said was, "Talk to you later."

Nick didn't turn around, just waved and kept going.

Paul and Brenda Crandall were watching a movie in the living room when Nick came in. He wanted to break all known speed records for getting through the front hall and up the stairs to his room, but his mom turned around as soon as she heard him, wearing the same big smile she gave him every time he came through that door.

Like she'd been saving up smiles like this her whole life.

"Hey, you," she said.

"Hey." Halfway up the stairs already.

"Have fun at the fair?" he heard from behind him.

"Yeah."

"I know this is probably a dumb question, after

an afternoon of junky fair food, but are you hungry? I'm going out in a little while, but I could fix you something right now if you want."

"No thanks." All the way at the top of the stairs now.

Closing the door behind him.

Trying to do what he had done behind closed doors just like this one a lot in his life: hope that tomorrow would be better.

Only right now, Nick couldn't make himself believe that, no matter how hard he tried.

He was quieter that night at dinner than he had been on all the other nights since baseball season had started. Or maybe dinner was quieter than usual because it was just his dad and him. His mom had left a few minutes ago for a book club meeting.

Finally his dad said, "Nick, is there something bothering you?"

Nick, keeping his head good and low over his food, said, "I'm fine."

Paul Crandall said, "Well, you don't act as if you're fine. Did something happen at the fair?"

Now Nick looked up. He could see his dad really wanted to know. But what good would it do to tell him the truth? Nick wasn't even sure a *baseball* dad would have been able to understand—or explain—what had really happened in front of that dunking booth today.

"It was nothing," Nick said, just managing to stop himself before he added "that you'd understand."

"Sounds like something to me."

Nick knew he wasn't going to get away with the silent treatment this time. So, knowing he wasn't telling it very well, he ran through the story as fast as he'd run away from that dunking booth.

The faster he talked, the less chance there was for him to start crying. That's the way he looked at it.

When Nick finished, his dad just sat there.

Paul Crandall said, "But it was just some silly game at the fair. Not a real one."

"That's just it," Nick said. "It *felt* like one," then added, "because a lot of the guys from the team were there. All week long they'd seen me make bad throws, and now with them all standing there, I couldn't make *any* kind of throw."

"But you're a wonderful thrower," his dad said. "I've seen it myself. I realize I'm no baseball expert—"

Tell me about it, Nick thought.

"—but one doesn't lose one's ability to throw in a single week."

"I did," Nick said.

"You're really being silly," his dad said. "It's not as if you've become a total failure at baseball in the span of a few short days."

"You're used to having all the answers, and you have no clue about this!" Nick yelled, slamming the table, rattling plates and glasses and silverware. "Like you have no clue about *me*!"

He couldn't help himself. Couldn't stop himself. It was as if everything that had been happening in baseball, everything that had happened all week at practice and now at the fair, came spilling out of him, spilling all over the table like water over the side of a tub, no way for him to stop it, even if he wanted to.

Which he didn't.

"You don't know anything about what it's like to

fail!" Nick said. Still yelling. "You're the one whose job it is to *tell* people when they're failing."

"Son, you're missing the point entirely—"

Paul Crandall looked to his left as if his wife were in her usual chair, like he was looking for her to help him out.

Or save him from not being able to understand his own son.

"Well, you don't have to tell *me* I'm failing," Nick said. "Failing at school, failing at baseball . . ."

The last part just came out, one last part of this he couldn't stop if he'd tried:

". . . failing at being your son."

For the second time that day, Nick ran.

ELEVEN

First varsity game, at home, against Valley Falls.

And even though the school day seemed to take twice as long as usual, it was finally, at long last, time for the top of the first.

Nick hadn't exactly thrown cheese during warm-ups. But he had done all right the few times he'd thrown down to Joey Johnson at second base.

At least I released the ball this time, Nick told himself after his first throw got to Joey on the fly.

Maybe I'm making progress.

His parents both had late classes today but said they'd try to make it for the last couple of innings. Gracie said she'd be there as soon as lacrosse practice was over. And of course Jack was there, Jack trying to relax Nick during warm-ups every chance he got.

"You want to know how I look at the whole situation?" Jack said while Nick was putting on his catching gear.

"Not really," Nick said.

"Well, I'm going to tell you, anyway."

"I was afraid of that."

Jack grinned. "Since the worst thing that probably will ever happen to you already happened at the fair," he said, "you've got no worries from here on out."

Nick stopped fastening his shin guards, looked up at him. "That's it?"

"It makes perfect sense, if you really think about it."

Nick laughed then, but not because he felt like it. Mostly he did it to make Jack feel better, because he knew Jack was trying to be the best friend he could possibly be.

When Nick was in full gear, Coach Williams came over and said, "Let's take a walk."

Nick left his glove and his mask on the bench, and the two of them walked along the first baseline toward right field.

"I know you don't think you're ready for this, but you are," Coach said.

"Their catcher is twice as big as me," Nick said.

"And probably has half your heart."

"I still can't throw."

"Anybody in this game today, including the pitchers, would kill to have an arm like yours. You just have to trust it, bud."

"I can't right now."

"Sure you can. You just gotta figure out a way to get *out* of your own way."

Over the coach's shoulder, he could see movement in the stands now, saw Gracie and some of her lacrosse teammates taking their seats in the bleachers. Gracie was still wearing her blue practice lacrosse jersey and had her Mavericks cap turned around backward on her head.

"I've got a friend who tells me that all the time," Nick said.

"He must be pretty smart," Coach said.

"She," Nick said.

Gary Watson struck out the side in the first inning, which meant that the only throws Nick had to make were back to Gary or down to Conor Bell at third when they'd throw the ball around after another one of the strikeouts.

A one-two-three inning.

Just like that, Nick was an official varsity baseball player.

Coach Williams was batting him ninth, last in the order. The game was still 0–0 when he finally came up in the bottom of the third, two runners on ahead of him, nobody out. His first varsity at-bat and he had to come up in a spot like this. And in a scoreless game. But when he looked down at Coach Williams in the third-base coach's box, he saw the bunt sign.

He wasn't being asked to knock in a run, just lay down a good bunt.

I can do that, Nick told himself.

If he sacrificed the runners over, the Tigers would have guys on second and third for Joey Johnson, their leadoff guy, one of the best hitters they had.

As the Valley pitcher, a lefty, went into his stretch position, Nick was already squaring around, bat level and out in front of him. The lefty cooperated by giving him a perfect pitch to bunt, belt high over the middle of the plate. Nick dropped the head of the bat slightly, caught the ball just where he wanted it, deadened it the way Coach Williams had been showing them—even put a little backhand on the sucker. The ball landed so softly near the first baseline it was as if Nick had tossed a rosin bag over there.

The only play the charging first baseman had was to tag Nick on his way by. Both runners moved up a base, and when Joey followed with a single, both of them scored. The Tigers were ahead 2–0.

Coach Williams came over to Nick at the end of the inning and bumped him some fist.

"*Great* play," Coach said.

"It was still just a bunt, Coach," Nick said. Thinking this was another time when the coach was making too big a deal out of something small he'd done.

"*Hey, look at me.*" Coach Williams's words came out fast and hot, surprising Nick.

He looked up at his coach.

"If there's one thing I know about you already, it's that you're a team guy," Coach said. "And you just executed a play perfectly that helped our team." Now he grinned at Nick, relaxing. "You're allowed to be happy is what I'm trying to say. Now, go get our pitcher through the top of the fourth so we hold on to the lead you just helped us get."

If only it had worked out that way.

It started with an error by Jack, who'd gone in to play second.

He made a nice stop on a ball hit to his right, going to his knees to get it on the backhand. But he rushed his throw, Steve Carberry couldn't dig the ball out of the dirt and Valley had only their second base runner of the game—their first since the second inning.

Nick knew the kid on first would be running.

The kid who'd singled in the second hadn't gotten a chance to try to steal because the batter after him had hit a perfect double-play ball. But now, as the next Valley batter stepped to the plate, his manager was yelling at him to wait for his pitch.

Nick looked down at the runner at first and was more convinced than ever: Guy was going.

Nick's heart was beating so hard he expected

to look down and see his chest protector flopping around.

The runner didn't take much of a lead right away. When Gary looked over his left shoulder, checking him, the kid moved even closer to the bag. But as soon as it was clear Gary was coming to the plate with the ball, Nick heard what sounded like everybody in the infield yelling at him at once.

"Going!"

The batter swung at the pitch, trying to protect his runner. It didn't slow Nick down even a little. He was on the move, up and out of his crouch, not feeling nervous at all in the moment, just feeling this was all stuff he'd done before, thinking only about making a decent throw.

Which he did.

The guy who couldn't even make a throw at the fair made one now, shocked himself with how much he had on the ball.

That wasn't the problem.

The problem was that the ball and the runner and Joey Johnson's glove all happened to arrive at second base at the exact same moment.

The kid sliding kicked up a ton of dirt, and Nick

couldn't tell at first what had happened. He just hoped that Joey had somehow made the grab, because his glove was still sitting right on top of the bag.

Only the ball wasn't in the glove.

It was rolling toward Les Roy, their center fielder, a kid from Jamaica who was easily the fastest player on their team. Les was charging fast now, fast enough to get to the ball and keep the guy at second.

It hadn't really been Nick's fault. He'd made a solid throw. Still, there the guy was anyway, nobody out.

Gary Watson came down to the foot of the mound, motioned for Nick to meet him there.

Not good.

"Get the ball *up* next time!" he said, putting his glove in front of his mouth the way the pitchers did on television when the catcher came out.

"I tried," Nick said.

"Try harder," Gary said. "I'm pitching my butt off out here."

Still steamed at Nick, he walked the next batter. Now Valley had two runners on base and, with their weak-hitting pitcher up at bat, they went for a double steal. Nick didn't need anybody to yell at him now. With a left-handed hitter at the plate, he could see the whole thing, knew his best shot was the guy going for third.

He got this throw up, all right.

Got it up and over Conor Bell's glove and over his head and down the left-field line.

Nick watched the ball from the plate, feeling totally helpless.

There was no outfield wall at Hayworth, just green grass that seemed to stretch forever as Nick's throw refused to stop rolling.

By the time it did, the game was tied at 2.

TWELVE

The walk to the bench when the inning ended, the game tied, felt longer to Nick than if he were walking all the way home.

He kept his head down, glove in his left hand, mask in his right. Forget about the sacrifice bunt. And about being a team player. He might as well have been playing for the *other* team, because he'd just plated two runs for them as if he'd knocked them in himself.

Coach Williams tried to be head cheerleader as usual. He patted Nick on the back, told him not to hang his head, told everybody not to hang *their* heads, that they were going to get Valley back, get the lead back, right now.

Rah, rah, Nick thought.

Then Gary Watson looked up from the opposite end of the bench from where Nick was sitting and said, "How are we going to do all that with *him* behind the plate?"

Coach Williams's head whipped around like it belonged to a character in one of Nick's comics. "Zip it, Gary. We're all on the same team here."

But this time Gary didn't back down or say what he really wanted to say under his breath. It was as if he wanted it all out in the open now, what he'd been thinking about Nick playing varsity the whole time.

"'Cept for the ones on the JV team," Gary said.

Coach Williams was up now, halfway between Gary and Nick, face red. "This might be our first game," he said, voice loud. "But this is the *last* time anybody on this team throws anybody else under the bus."

Nick sat there more embarrassed than ever, less a part of the team than ever. Thinking, If I tried to throw somebody under the bus, I'd probably screw that up, too.

● ● ●

Valley stole bases on him the next two innings. But it happened with two outs both times, and neither one of the guys scored because Gary ended both innings with strikeouts.

Nick managed to get the ball to Joey on the fly both times, even if they were sad-looking, lollipop throws that had no chance of beating the runners. And the *really* sad part was that Nick didn't care what the throws looked like, he was just happy that he hadn't thrown the ball away.

Some team guy.

They played seven-inning games in varsity, unless the game ran late. No inning could start after five-thirty. But the Hayworth-Valley game was moving along, staying at 2–2, even though both teams had had chances to take the lead. Nick's second time up, there had been a runner on third and one out, and he'd hit a fly ball to left he was sure would be deep enough to be a sacrifice fly.

But Conor Bell, the runner on third, had started home when the ball was hit, thinking it might fall, and by the time he went back to tag, the Valley left fielder already had the ball in his glove. Conor tried to come home even with his late break, but the throw beat him easily, and the game was still tied.

In the bottom of the sixth, though, Joey doubled and Gary singled him home, and Hayworth went to the seventh inning ahead 3–2.

As Nick and Gary were walking onto the field, Gary came up and patted him on the back, the way Coach would.

That was what it must have looked like to the rest of the team, anyway. But what Gary whispered into Nick's ear was this:

"Try not to mess this up before we get out of here with a W."

Then he patted Nick one more time and headed for the mound. Nick didn't know whether it was unusual or not for Gary to get the chance to pitch a complete game, but Coach had said that his pitch count was low, and so it was his game to win or lose.

It had taken less than a week for Gary Watson to turn into Nick's archenemy. Like Black Adam was for Captain Marvel. Still: As Nick took Gary's warm-up throws, he was thinking he'd never rooted for a pitcher harder in his life—not even with the

Mets or Yankees—than he was rooting for Gary Watson right now.

Because if he could strike out the side one last time, the Tigers would win their opener, which would mean Nick hadn't lost it.

Gary still had plenty of arm left. He proceeded to strike out the first two Valley batters in the bottom of the seventh.

But then, out of nowhere, because pitchers could lose it that fast, he began struggling with his control. He walked the next batter on four pitches. And the next.

Tying run at second, go-ahead run at first, game still on.

Normally Nick would have gone out to the mound and tried to relax his pitcher. Just not now. Not with this pitcher. When Nick looked out at Gary, he imagined a moat between them, like you'd see in front of a castle.

Coach Williams didn't come out to the mound, either. He'd said it was Gary's game to win or lose, and now it really was.

On the first pitch to the next batter, the Valley cleanup hitter, Gary threw what Nick thought was a perfect fastball, one with some late break to it that ended up in exactly the right spot, low and on the outside corner.

The guy just got a piece of it, and rolled it toward Conor Bell at third. The problem was that Conor, with two outs in the last inning, had been playing back, not just back but on the line, guarding against an extra-base hit. Long way for him to come in. He still managed to get a good jump on the ball, darting forward as soon as he saw how slowly it had come off the bat, barehanding it like a pro, whipping a sidearm throw to Steve Carberry that would have gotten the runner by a step—if it had been on target.

It wasn't.

The throw was wide. *Way* wide.

Like one of mine, Nick thought.

It was wide right, Steve's right. As soon as it was past him, it was going to roll the way Nick's wild throw to Conor had. And when this baby stopped rolling, Valley was going to be ahead.

And that's what would have happened—exactly—except for one thing: Nick was there, backing up the play.

He had sprinted toward first with the Valley cleanup hitter, the way he'd been taught long before he ever got to varsity. Not only did he beat the runner to the bag, he kept right on going as he followed Conor's throw, diving full-out for it as it went past Steve, feeling the ball hit the pocket of his catcher's mitt.

As soon as Nick knew he had the ball, he scrambled to his feet and saw that the runner from second had rounded third and was halfway home.

From behind first, Nick instinctively knew he had no shot at that runner.

But he did have a clear shot at the cleanup guy, who had been so sure the throw was long gone that he'd rounded the bag hard.

The Valley kid coaching first saw Nick with the ball and screamed at his runner, "Get back!"

Too late. The runner had too much momentum.

He managed to skid to a stop, dove back for the bag just as Nick dove at *him*. The ball out of his mitt and in his bare hand now. Nick put the ball between the kid's hand and first base, getting a faceful of dirt, what felt like a whole *infield's* worth of dirt, at the same time.

The field ump made the call at first.

"Out!"

The home plate ump saw that Nick had tagged the runner before the kid coming from third had crossed home plate.

It all meant that Hayworth had won, 3–2.

Nick was still lying there in the dirt near first base when Coach Williams and Jack Elmore got to him at pretty much the same time, telling him the game was over.

"When I talked about needing your right arm," Coach Williams said, "I didn't mean like *this*."

At least it's still good for something, Nick thought.

THIRTEEN

At Wiffle ball the next day, all Nick's JV team-mates—the guys he still thought of as his real team-mates—wanted to talk about the play that ended the Valley Falls game.

"I heard you extended your arm like you were Mr. Fantastic," Zach Dugas said, referring to the guy who could stretch himself as far as he wanted in the *Fantastic Four* movies.

Jeff Kantor said, "We'd compare you to the daughter in *The Incredibles* if, you know, she wasn't a girl."

"Thanks so much," Nick said. "That's *exactly* who I always wanted to be. I can't believe I don't have a poster of her up in my room, now that I think about it." Nick put his hands together as if he were praying. "And you guys can cut it out. Please."

He was serious. That play was just one out in a game full of them, and Nick knew it. It wasn't as if he'd won the game all by himself.

Coach Williams liked to talk about how one bounce of the ball could change everything in sports. Yesterday, Nick was the one who ended up bouncing in the right direction on the last play of the game.

In his mind, it still didn't make him a varsity player, didn't make him feel as if he were a part of that team.

And it sure didn't change anything else going on in his life right now. One lucky play wasn't exactly like being able to say "Shazam!"

His dad didn't want to hear about baseball that night at dinner. He had something else on his mind—and something else on the dinner table: some printouts, stacked neatly next to his plate.

Nick didn't have a good feeling about them, judging from the expression on his dad's face, but somehow he knew it was up to him to ask about them.

"What are those?" he said.

"Why don't you tell me?" his dad said, sliding them across the table.

They were e-mails from Nick's teachers.

"In fact, why don't you read them?" Paul Crandall said. "Aloud."

Nick did, mumbling until his dad told him to speak up. They all said pretty much the same thing about what a bright young man he was and how well liked he was by his classmates but how he wasn't spending enough time on his homework.

What they all described as "out-of-class" work.

"At least you're consistent," Paul Crandall said. "I'll give you that."

"Wish I could be this consistent behind the plate," Nick said, trying to lighten the mood a little.

"This has nothing to do with baseball," his dad said. "Except in this one way: You are on notice, as of right now, about your work habits at school. Because if they do not improve between now and the end of the school year, you're not playing town baseball this summer. Maybe in other summers you thought of baseball as your right. This summer, it will be treated somewhat differently, as a privilege."

"But—"

"There are no buts," his dad said. "Or ands, or ifs, for that matter. The time for talking about all this is over, Nick. It's time for action."

Nick felt as helpless as he did watching that throw of his disappear over Conor's head.

"It's not fair," he said.

Sometimes his mom would come to the rescue during one of these conversations.

Not this time.

"I have to support your father in this," she said. "We both just want you to find the best in yourself, in everything you do."

"It means in the classroom as well as on the baseball field," his dad said.

"I'm trying."

"Try harder," his dad said.

Sounding exactly like Gary Watson.

There was nothing more to say. Nick didn't feel like having dessert, just went straight upstairs and did his homework, even though he wasn't any more interested in it tonight than any other night.

His parents took turns checking on him. Each time, they found Nick either sitting at his desk or on the floor with his homework papers scattered around him.

The last time his dad came up, he said to Nick, "When you're finished with your assignments, you can read comics if you want, until lights-out."

Nick didn't look up from the floor. "Thanks," he said.

"We *are* doing this for your own good," his dad said. "You *can* do this work."

Nick kept scribbling away, just wanting his dad to leave the room.

He was tired of getting pep talks. Tired of everything. When baseball had started—JV baseball—he didn't want the school year to end. Now he couldn't wait for it to be over.

When he finally finished his English assignment, took the notes he'd been scribbling for his book report and typed them out on his laptop, he went into his box of comics, like the big old box that Mr. Boyd used to have, and picked out a DC Comics Presents called *Superman and Shazam!*

On the cover, Superman is wearing Captain Marvel's costume, and Captain Marvel is wearing Superman's.

Superman says, "Cap! What's the idea of switching costumes with me?"

And the Captain says, "I've gained all your powers, too, Superman! While I wear this costume I'm you—and you're me!"

They were lucky.

Nick didn't know who he was anymore.

FOURTEEN

The second game of the season, against Thayer
Academy, went worse than the first, at least for
Nick.

Conor Bell was their starting pitcher this time,
and even though Nick thought Conor had solid stuff,
it wasn't close to Gary Watson's. Conor couldn't
throw as hard and didn't have the same control. It
meant more hits, more walks, more base runners.

More chances to steal.

And the Thayer runners were stealing. At will.

Conor wasn't helping, because he had so much
motion in his windup that he seemed to take twice
as much time as Gary delivering the ball to the
plate. Even with that, Nick knew in his heart that
even if Conor had one of those slide steps that big-
league pitchers used when there were runners on

base, even if he were following it up with a hundred-mile-per-hour fastball, Thayer's guys would have still looked as happy as kids running around a playground at recess.

They stole two bases on him in the first, three in the second, three more in the third. The only time Nick got an out on any of them was when a Thayer runner overslid second base, and Joey—who'd had to jump to keep another one of Nick's throws from going over his head—came down with this sweet move and put the tag on the kid before he could scramble back.

That was in the top of the third. The Tigers were behind 5–0 by then. And by the time Thayer's half of the inning ended, they had tacked on two more runs.

Nick caught up with Conor before he got to their bench and apologized for what felt like the tenth time today already.

"Relax, dude," Conor said. "Those guys aren't putting themselves on base."

"But I keep giving them extra bases," Nick said.

"Listen," Conor said, "if I ever start throwing

the ball better, maybe you won't have to throw it at all. Okay?"

"Okay."

Since he'd come to the varsity, Nick had felt like he only had two guys watching his back, Coach Williams and Jack Elmore. Now he felt like he could add Conor Bell to the list.

Once it was 7–0 for Thayer, though, the game started to run. The more tired the Thayer pitcher got, the more he lost his control. The harder he tried to fix that—by aiming the ball—the more it looked as if he needed MapQuest to find home plate. The Tigers suddenly had base runners, lots of base runners, and they were running, and stealing, on the Thayer catcher the way the Thayer runners had been stealing against Nick.

The Tigers wound up getting four runs in the fourth—Nick scoring one of them after he'd walked—and four more in the fifth to take the lead. All those runs seemed to relax Conor, who finally started throwing the way he wanted to. He finished his day with three perfect innings before giving way to his bullpen for the top of the seventh. And even though Les Roy, their number-three pitcher, loaded the bases with two outs in the seventh, the Tigers got out of there with an 8–7 victory.

Somehow, despite Nick and his horrible throwing, the Tigers were 2–0 on the season. If they could win their next game, against Maumee Valley, they would go into their rivalry game against King undefeated.

King had three times as many students as Hayworth, even *recruited* good players in all sports to go there. Not only did they always win their league, they had beaten Hayworth ten straight times.

Not only that, but King's catcher was a kid named Zane Diaz, and everybody who played ball in their area had heard of him. He lived in Sherrill, the next town over, and had been on the Little League All-Star team from there that had made it all the way to the semifinals of the Little League World Series in Williamsport two years before. Everybody had gotten to see him play on ESPN.

Zane Diaz was not only big and strong and had a ton of left-handed power as a hitter, he could throw the ball to second from his *knees*. Nick had seen him do it during a Babe Ruth game last summer.

And yet.

And yet from the first day of practice, Coach Williams had been telling his players that the sides were even this time. And although the Tigers had only managed to win two games so far, both by one run, Nick could see the other varsity players starting to believe.

"Last year they beat us 15–0," Jack Elmore said. "But this ain't last year."

"Yeah, but remember something," Nick said, sounding as sarcastic as he could. "We've got a secret weapon this year—me and my total inability to throw out base runners. Watch out, King, and watch out, world."

"Hey," Jack said. "We won today, right? Because you act as if we were the ones who blew the 7–0 lead."

Nick knew Jack was right.

It was still not hard to feel as if he had blown it, too.

Nick and Gracie were sitting in the circle waiting for Gracie's mom to drive them home, since Nick's mom and dad had had to rush back to their school for a faculty meeting.

"Why so quiet, Captain?" Gracie said. "Our team won today."

"No thanks to me," Nick said.

"What's that supposed to mean?" Gracie said.

"Do you really want to know?"

"Wouldn't have asked if I didn't."

And it all came out of him then, everything he'd been feeling for the last week or so, some of which he'd already talked about with Gracie, some not. Came out of him the way it had with his dad that night at dinner.

"I don't belong with these guys," he said. "On the varsity, I mean. And just because we won today doesn't change that. We won in spite of me, not because of me. The whole team knows that. Coach Williams has to know that by now, he just won't admit it."

He waited for Gracie to say something. When she didn't, he kept going.

"I used to love baseball," he said. "More than comics, more than anything. But it's not fun any-more, and now I feel more lost than I ever have, because if I don't at least belong on a baseball field,

I don't belong anywhere. And I *sure* don't belong with my mom and dad. They don't know what to make of me any more than I know what to make of them."

He stopped now, took a breath, closed his eyes, felt the heat and sting of the tears he'd been doing his best to hold back for a week.

Just then he saw Mrs. Wright's car coming up the drive from Frogtown Road.

When Nick opened his eyes, he saw Gracie staring at him.

"To be continued," she said.

She didn't say anything on the ride home, just stared out the back window. Nick didn't say anything, either. When they got out of the car, Nick, seeing that his parents weren't home yet, started walking toward Gracie's front door.

But she stopped him.

"Let's go around back for a few minutes," Gracie said.

"Okay," Nick said. "But why?"

"Now there's something *I* need to talk to *you* about."

"Sounds important."

"That's why we need to go to the swings," Gracie said.

They walked around the side of her house and back to where the swings were, the place where they'd always done their best and most serious talking from the first day they'd known each other.

Nick sat down first and said, "Okay, Miss Mysterious, what do you want to talk about?"

"About how you've turned into the biggest baby I know."

She didn't sit down in the swing next to his, the way she usually did when they were out here kicking things around. She just stood in front of him, hands on her hips, and let him have it.

"I can't figure out what's worse," Gracie said, "how dumb you've gotten about sports, or how *totally* dumb you are about your mom and dad."

"You don't get it," Nick said.

"No, *you* don't get it," she said.

"Get what?"

"What an idiot you've turned into."

Nick felt the way you did when the other pitcher was coming with high heat.

"Hold on—"

"No," Gracie said, "*you* hold on. I've been listening to you complain for weeks. Now you listen to me."

He did.

"First question," she said. "When did you become such an expert on being a parent? Seriously. You know how many kids we go to school with every single day who have parents who take no interest in anything they're doing, either 'cause they're too busy or just don't want to be bothered? I'll tell you how many, Captain: a lot."

In a quiet voice Nick said, "I didn't say they don't care."

"This isn't about caring," Gracie said. "My parents care about me. But do you see them showing up for all my lacrosse games? My dad hasn't been to one yet."

Nick sat there.

"It was a *pain* for your parents to get here for your game today, then have to leave the minute it was over. But guess what? They were there. They made the effort. You know how I know that? I did this amazing thing—I talked to them. You should try it sometime."

"I do try talking to them. They're just so mad different from me."

"Well boo *hoo*," she said. "You think all parents aren't that way? You don't think all kids don't think their parents are from Mars? How totally thick are you? You know what you need to do? Get your head out of your comic books once in a while and look at what you've got instead of whining about what you don't have."

No stopping her now, no slowing her down. Nick waited for steam to come pouring out of her.

All heat.

"You ever hear the saying 'you can pick your friends but not your family'? Well, guess what? Your family chose *you*. They could have picked anybody to be a luckier-than-any-foster-kid-in-the-world kid. And they chose *you,* Crandall. They're trying to learn about baseball because of *you.* They're trying to get you to be better in school—which, Earth to Nick, you should be—because they want the best for *you*."

"That's what *they* say."

"*And guess what?*" She was really yelling now. "They're right!"

Gracie turned and pointed across the street at his house. "You told me yourself one time, when you were living in that apartment with the Boyds, you always dreamed about a house like this in a neighborhood like this. A real home with parents inside who'd love you the way your mom and dad do. So they don't love baseball the way you do. Another boo hoo. My dad loves me to death, and he doesn't even know what *position* I play in lacrosse. I mean, what planet are you living on?"

Gracie started to walk back toward the house, as if she were done. But halfway across the backyard, she turned around and nearly ran back at him, like she was going to tackle him in the open field.

"I almost told you this in the car, but I didn't want to say it in front of my mom," Gracie said. "But you've spent so much time in your life feeling sorry for yourself, you don't know when it's time to stop."

FIFTEEN

Gary Watson was so dominating against Maumee Valley that Nick never had a chance to jam things up for him.

He gave up just one hit, struck out ten, and the Tigers won, 10–0.

When the Maumee Valley center fielder got his team's only hit, a single in the fourth, Joey and Jack promptly turned a 4–6–3 double play to take him off the bases. By the time Gary got around to walking two guys in the top of the last inning, there was no point in either of them trying to steal—they were too far behind.

Nick even got a hit, on a day when everybody who started for the Tigers got a hit, but he wasn't thinking about that when the game was over. What he was thinking about was how he hadn't made any bad throws and how that made the day a total success almost as much as the final score did.

Now it was Friday, and the big game against King was coming up on Monday. Nick was upstairs in his room, even on a Friday night, doing homework—he'd been trying to do better with that since Gracie had lit into him—when he heard a knock on his wall.

He looked up. It was his dad, wearing jeans and an old green Dartmouth sweatshirt and his one pair of sneakers, tennis shoes that Nick always thought were as old as his dad was.

"Glad to see you hitting the books," his dad said. "How close are you to being done?"

"Pretty close."

"Well, when you are, come on downstairs, there's something I want to show you."

This was one of those nights when Nick was stretched out on the floor, papers all around him, his signature studying position. He looked up now and said, "Please tell me it's not more e-mails from my teachers."

"No, it's not," he said. "Just come downstairs when you're finished working."

Nick worked for ten more minutes on math, closed his book, stacked up his worksheets and went downstairs to the living room.

When he got there he couldn't believe his eyes.

Paul Crandall was sitting on the couch, pounding his fist into a brand-new Wilson baseball glove, black with a brown pocket.

"Dad, I don't need a new glove. And, besides, I'm a catcher, remember?"

"The glove isn't for you." His dad grinned. "It's for me."

"You bought yourself a glove?"

"Be logical, son," Paul Crandall said. "How can we play catch if I don't have a glove?"

After just a few minutes in the yard, Nick wasn't worried about making accurate throws anymore. He was a lot more worried that one of them might send his dad to the hospital.

Even his softest throw seemed to be hitting his dad everywhere except his new glove.

"Remember when I mentioned that I wasn't

perfect?" Paul Crandall said at one point, an embarrassed smile on his face.

Coaches always told you to try to aim the ball at the middle of the other guy's chest. Trouble was, when Nick managed to pull that off, the ball would actually hit his dad in the chest.

"I'm a little out of practice, as you can see," his dad said as he reached over to pick up another ball he'd just dropped.

"You'll get it," Nick said. Sounding like the dad here, not the kid.

Amazingly, Paul Crandall was as bad—and awkward—throwing the ball as he was trying to catch it. When his dad threw the ball back, he bounced it in front of Nick the way Nick had been bouncing balls in front of varsity fielders all season.

"I probably should have started doing this a little sooner," his dad said. "Say about 1952."

Nick smiled then, a smile he couldn't have stopped if he'd tried. "Tonight's fine," he said. He held the ball for a second. "But can I ask you a question?"

"I just hope answering it isn't as hard for me as this game of catch is turning out to be."

"Why tonight?" Nick said.

"I'll be honest with you," he said. "Your mother and I had a bit of a discussion the other night. Well, technically, it was more her talking and me listening. And what she told me is that maybe it was time for *me* to do more than talk a good game when it came to baseball, because that's what dads are supposed to do with their sons."

"I had the same sort of . . . *discussion* with Gracie," Nick said.

"About baseball?"

Nick said, "About everything."

"Anyway," his dad said, "here I am."

"I'm glad," Nick said.

"Me too."

They kept playing catch in what daylight they had left. Paul Crandall didn't turn into a Gold Glover while they did. But he didn't quit, no matter how many times Nick saw him wince in pain after he'd demanded Nick start throwing the ball harder, throwing it as if he meant it.

And his dad did get a little better the longer they stayed out there.

Nick was so focused on his dad, so focused on

giving him throws he could handle, even aiming them so they ended up on his glove side, a little away from his body, that it didn't occur to him until afterward that the ball was ending up where he was aiming it almost every single time.

What did occur to Nick Crandall while they were out in the yard was this: It wasn't just a house like this, on a street like this that he had imagined when he was still in foster care. It had been a *night* exactly like this.

Not playing ball with the world's greatest baseball dad.

Just his own.

SIXTEEN

When they were inside, Nick decided this was as good a time as any to show his dad something, too.

"A present I bought," Nick said. "With my own money. For myself."

They went up to his room, and he opened the top drawer of his desk and took out the book:

King Arthur and the Knights of the Round Table.

He'd bought it at the Hayworth book fair the day after Gracie had yelled at him.

It had *Great Illustrated Classics* printed across the top of the cover, over a drawing of King Arthur and some of his knights, and it was written by a guy named Howard Pyle. For a used copy, Nick thought it was in pretty decent shape.

Paul Crandall stared at the book, then back at Nick.

"You were right," Nick said. "It *is* one of the great stories in the history of stories."

"For boys of all ages," his dad said, gently taking the book out of Nick's hands now, opening to where it was bookmarked. "And I see you're well into it."

"I've been reading a little of it every night the past few nights," Nick said. He grinned and said, "Maybe under the covers sometimes with that book light Mom got me."

"I seem to recall another boy who used to do the exact same thing," Paul Crandall said, "at about your exact same age."

The two of them sat down on the bed, his dad still holding the book.

His dad said, "What made you get it?"

"Kind of a long story," Nick said. "But not nearly as good as this one."

Nick didn't tell him how he'd gone home that night from the swings and realized he had turned into a baby. How he added things up—not needing a worksheet this time—and realized that if one bad slump in baseball was the worst thing that ever happened to him, his life wasn't just good.

It was great.

He didn't tell his dad any of that, just said to him, "I figured it was about time for me to do something more than talk a good game about books."

Then Nick and his dad were talking about King Arthur and Lancelot and Merlin and Queen Guinevere, Nick telling his dad he couldn't believe it once he got into the book, how much Merlin reminded him of the old wizard guy who gave Billy Batson his power in Captain Marvel. How he had no idea that Arthur pulling the sword out of the stone when he was a kid was just the beginning of the cool stuff that would happen later.

"*Very* cool stuff," his dad said.

Nick loved how Lancelot was kind of an orphan himself, and how he was just getting to the parts about how Lancelot and King Arthur were fighting over Guinevere.

"I can't believe it," Nick said. "All that over a girl?"

"Well, not just *any* old girl," his dad said. "Think of her as a Gracie-type girl."

"Still," Nick said. "Going to war?"

His dad patted him on the shoulder and said, "You'll understand when you're older. Hopefully not as old as me."

"You weren't old playing ball tonight," Nick said.

His dad laughed out loud now, the kind of laugh Nick hardly ever heard from him, and said, "Well, you're nice to say so."

Just then they heard the doorbell ring. Nick's mom was calling upstairs a minute later, saying it was Coach Williams to see Nick.

Coach Williams was there to tell him that Bobby Mazzilli's wrist had healed and that he'd been cleared to play.

SEVENTEEN

Paul and Brenda Crandall left them alone in the living room, Coach Williams on the couch and Nick facing him from a chair on the other side of the coffee table.

Feeling like he'd been called to the principal's office but not sure why.

This was the chair he sat in when he and his dad had some of their talks about his schoolwork.

"Bobby was probably ready to practice a couple of days ago," Coach Williams was saying. "But he had one last doctor's appointment today. And I frankly didn't want him putting any more pressure on you than you were already feeling by hanging around practice."

"Yeah," Nick said.

"He's been working out with his dad, though, on his own."

Bobby's dad, Nick knew, was the varsity coach at the high school.

Nick just waited, hands on his knees. He noticed that he could already see them turning into catcher's hands, a little lumpy in some places. He was staring at his hands because he didn't know what to think about this, what to say. If Coach had told him a few days ago that Bobby was ready to reclaim his old job, Nick would have been relieved.

Happy, even.

Not now.

"I told Bobby not to say anything to anybody until I had a chance to talk to you," Coach Williams said. "I'm the one who got you into this, after all."

Nick said, "I don't know what I'm supposed to say."

Coach Williams took a deep breath, let it out. "I'm not going to lie to you, Nick. I feel like I've been honest with you from the start, and I'm gonna be honest now. Once Bobby's good to go, I'm gonna send you back to JV, where you can play every game and get ready for next season. You know that's best, right?"

Nick nodded. It was pretty amazing, if you thought about it, how often grown-ups told you what was best for you.

"One small problem," Coach Williams said. "The big game on Monday."

"The biggest," Nick said.

"This is our year to get those guys," Coach Williams said. "We've finally got players who aren't just good enough to do it, but believe they can do it." He took another deep breath and said, "What I'm here to find out is if you're one of those players. Bobby thinks he's ready right now to be the starting catcher on the Hayworth team that finally beats King. What about you, Nick?"

Nick wanted Gracie here. Or his dad. Or his mom.

But he knew this was on him.

He knew he was the one being challenged here.

It was completely quiet in the house. Since he'd been called up to varsity—adopted again, that's what he'd told Gracie—he'd been looking for a way out, a way to get off the team and get back to JV.

Now here that chance was, staring him right in the face.

All he had to do was say the word.

So he did.

"I want to play," Nick said.

Coach Williams smiled.

"All I wanted to know," he said.

EIGHTEEN

King's nickname was the Vikings, and Nick thought that worked out just fine, because it looked to him as if a few of their guys were big enough to play for the *Minnesota* Vikings.

The pro football team.

The biggest of them was Zane Diaz, star catcher.

"I know who I want to be when I grow up," Jack Elmore said to Nick while the Vikings were finishing up with infield, pointing out at Zane. "Him."

Nick said, "Even his catcher's mitt looks small on him."

"Well," Jack said, "you know what they say: Bigger they are, harder they fall."

Just then Zane Diaz cut loose with a throw down to second base. With what looked like just a small flick of his wrist, he nearly took the glove off his second baseman's hand.

"*Who* says that?" Nick said.

He had told himself that his attitude was going to be completely different today, his last game on the varsity—for now—no matter what. No hanging his head, no worrying what he might do to lose this game, focusing instead, every chance he got, on ways to win it.

Basically, he was going to be a different guy.

But how did he do that going up against a guy like Zane Diaz?

Coach Williams must have seen him staring at Zane, because he came down and sat next to him.

"Remember something," he said. "We're not just playing their catcher today. We're playing the whole King team."

"Coach," Nick said quietly, "that guy is *awesome*."

"Just play your game," Coach Williams said. "A pitch at a time, an out at a time, an inning at a time. And before you know it, it'll be a day you'll remember the rest of your life."

He had thrown well during warm-ups, as well

as he had yet, hadn't babied the ball. It was part of his new attitude. If he was going to make a mistake today, he wasn't going to make one because he was afraid.

Before he took his position behind the plate to start the game, he looked up to the top row of the stands where his dad and mom and Gracie were sitting. His parents both gave him small waves, looking more nervous to Nick, even from this far away, than Nick felt.

Gracie, though, was smiling her head off, as if there was no other place in the world she'd rather be than watching Hayworth vs. King. Right before the ump told them to play ball, she stood up and waved at Nick.

At first he thought she was pointing to her heart.

She wasn't.

Nick smiled back.

The game was 2–2 by the third, the two King runs coming on a massive two-run homer from Zane Diaz that went over Les Roy's head in center and seemed as if it might not come to a stop until it made it all the way to the JV field. By the time Les had chased the ball down and gotten it back to Joey Johnson—who went all the way out to Les's normal position to take the cutoff throw—Zane was already across home plate.

The guy scoring ahead of Zane on the home run, their first baseman, was still on base with two outs because Nick *hadn't* thrown him out trying to steal second.

King wasn't a fast team, and it was the first base they'd tried to steal. And Nick's throw, one that could have ended the inning right there and made Zane lead off the fourth, was decent. It was just a little too high. Joey made a nice catch, got the tag on the kid, but he got him on his hip, and a half second late.

Because there were enough days between the Tigers' last game and this one, Gary Watson was on the mound. Zane Diaz crushed the next pitch he saw from him after the steal, and the game was tied, just like that.

The next inning, though, with a runner on third and two outs, Nick redeemed himself.

He picked up a slow roller down the third

baseline, a ball neither Gary nor Conor Bell had a chance to get to, dropping to one knee, then side-arming the ball as hard as he could toward Steve Carberry.

At the other end of the play, Steve made the best stretch Nick had seen him make all season, the runner was out and the game stayed at 2–2.

Jack, who hadn't gone in to play second yet, was the first to get to him when he reached the bench.

"That wasn't just money," he yelled. "Dude, that was *allowance* money!"

Before Nick could say anything back, Steve Carberry came jogging by, ducked his head, bumped Nick's mitt with his own. "Throw," he said.

Nick wanted to do more than throw in the top of the fifth, when he came up with runners on second and third, nobody out, King ahead now 3–2. But the best he could do was a hard ground ball right back at the pitcher, who held the runners and threw him out. Two batters later, though, Gary singled both guys home, and Hayworth was ahead of King, 4–3.

It stayed that way into the top of the seventh.

Three outs away.

Tomorrow, Nick knew, Bobby Mazzilli would be the starting catcher.

And Nick would be back with JV.

Just not now.

Gary Watson hadn't struck out as many guys as he usually did today, but that was one of the reasons why his pitch count was low again, why he was still in there for the top of the last inning.

Before they all took the field, Coach Williams called his team around around him in front of their bench.

"I'll keep this short," he said. "Hopefully, you'll all go on to play bigger games than this in your lives. Then he looked from face to face, trying to smile at every one of them as he said, "You just won't be playing one bigger today."

He put his hand out, and they all crowded in to put theirs on top of it.

"Now, go beat those guys," he said.

King's shortstop singled to start the seventh. Gary was so focused on getting the next batter that he completely forgot about the runner, who got a huge jump on him. When Gary yelled "no throw," Nick held the ball.

Stolen base.

The runner moved over to third when the next kid grounded out to second.

One out, runner on third.

Gary put everything he had left into getting the next batter, striking out the King pitcher on three pitches.

Just like that, the Tigers were one out away, the tying run still at third.

Gary walked the next batter, not getting the call from the home plate ump on a close 3–2 pitch. But that wasn't such a bad thing, because the following batter was the weakest King had, the smallest kid on their team, one who'd gone in to play second back in the fourth inning after their regular second baseman had hurt himself sliding into third.

Gary had struck him out on three pitches his first time up. Before he stepped in now, Gary motioned for Nick to come out to the mound, something he'd only done one other time.

The message hadn't changed.

"The only way we can lose from here is if somebody messes up," he said, "because this guy has *no* chance."

They both knew he didn't mean "somebody."

To the end he wasn't giving an inch.

"So don't let the ball get by you," Gary said. "And if they send the runner from first, let him go. I'm going to get a strikeout whether it's first-and-third or second-and-third. Got it?"

"Got it," Nick said.

Only Gary Watson didn't strike the kid out. He tried so hard—too hard—to throw the perfect pitch that he overthrew the first one and came in so low and so far inside that it hit the kid on the foot.

Bases loaded now.

Still one out away if Gary could get it.

Problem was, the out would have to be Zane Diaz.

Nick looked over at the King bench. They had all turned their caps inside out, rally-cap style, and they were pounding on each other as if Zane had cleared the bases already. Zane, a lefty, was three-for-three already. Home run, double, single. Had scorched the ball all three times.

Maybe we should walk him, Nick thought. Let the tying run score, take our chances with the next guy.

Even though Coach Williams had come out to talk to Gary, tried to calm him down, you could see that Gary was still thinking about the pitch that had clipped the second baseman.

The count went to 2–0, both pitches high and outside, not even close to being strikes.

Nick stood up then, trying to slow things down, not just Gary, slow the whole game down, acting as if he were checking his infielders, as if he might move them around.

For some reason, he took one last look up in the bleachers, to where Gracie was standing along with everybody else. Took one last look at what she had written in red Magic Marker on the front of her white T-shirt, what had made him smile at her before the first pitch.

Shazam.

Yeah, he thought.

Then he looked away from Gracie and straight at Jack Elmore.

It all happened fast after that. Gary Watson threw ball three, another one high and outside, but Nick didn't care, he wasn't worried about the count or about Zane. He was stepping out in front of Zane and away from the plate at the same time so Gary Watson wasn't in the line of fire.

Because it wasn't the pitcher's game to win or lose now.

It was the catcher's.

Jack Elmore was in, playing second, and he cut behind the runner at second, who'd been taking a bigger and more careless lead with each pitch. Cut behind him as if he'd been able to read Nick's mind when Nick looked at him.

Nick threw the ball as hard as he could, as hard as he'd ever thrown a ball, threw it to the shortstop side, right where he'd aimed it.

Right where Jack's glove was now.

The runner slid right into it, and the field umpire crouched there threw his arm up into the air and yelled "Out!" as if he wanted people down on Frogtown Road to be able to hear him.

Hayworth 4, King 3.

Final.

"Shazam," Nick said quietly at home plate as everything got real loud around him.

Zane Diaz was still standing there, bat in his hand, as if he couldn't believe what he'd just seen, what had just happened. "What did you say?" he said.

And Nick said, "Just talking to myself."

"That's as much arm as I've seen all season, dude," Zane Diaz said, and bumped Nick some fist.

Somehow, through the rest of the players, Gracie got to him first, asking if he could see her T-shirt, could he really? And Nick said, yeah, he saw the shirt, right from the start. Then his parents were there along with Gracie, Nick's dad grabbing him and saying into his ear, "Not just a knight today. A king, in just about every way."

When Nick finally broke loose from his dad, there was Coach Williams.

"Nice throw," he said, putting his hand out.

"Thanks," Nick said.

Coach Williams paused then, still holding on to Nick's right hand, and said, "See you next season, kid."

"I'll be here," Nick said.

And then Gracie Wright was trying her very best to sound like the announcer in the Disney commercials you saw after the Super Bowl.

"Nick Crandall," she said, "now that you've won the big game over King, where are you going next?"

Nick looked down at the plate, then up at his mom and dad.

"Home," he said.

Turn the page for a preview of
Mike Lupica's next novel,

LONG SHOT

ONE

Pedro Morales loved playing basketball with Ned Hancock.

It didn't make Pedro different from any other sixth-grade basketball player at Vernon Middle School. Or in the whole town of Vernon for that matter. Ned made everybody around him better, every time he stepped on a court, whether it was for a real game or just scrimmaging.

But the thing Pedro liked best about playing with Ned is that Ned made *him* better.

Ned was doing that for him now, in the pickup game they were playing in the gym at the middle school. Which in their town, because the school district was so big, was for sixth-graders only. A school all their own is the way they looked at it, no seventh- or eighth-graders to bother them or bully them or bigtime them.

Today the kids had the gym all to themselves, school having been dismissed early because of teacher conferences. But Mr. Lucchino, the principal, had offered to stick around and let them use the gym, knowing that the first practice for the town team was the following Wednesday night, now that the players had been selected.

Pedro, a point guard, was on Ned's team today. Ned had picked him first even though he could have gone for a bigger guy. Ned liked playing with Pedro, too, because Pedro could pass. Not as well as Ned could. Nobody their age in Vernon could do anything in basketball as well as Ned could.

But Ned always wanted guys around him who knew how to pass. Even though he was only eleven years old, it was as if he already knew exactly how basketball was meant to be played. And that started with moving the ball.

Pedro felt the same way. Playing with Ned, going back to last year when they were old enough to play on their first town team together, reminded him why he loved basketball so much, loved it the way his father, who had been a star soccer player as a boy in Mexico, had always wanted him to love soccer.

Now the game Pedro and the rest of his friends were playing—first to ten baskets, didn't have to win by two—was tied at 9–all. Pedro's team had the ball. As they were taking it out under their basket, Ned said to Pedro, "Let's do this."

Ned was serious. It wasn't a pickup game to him now. If they were keeping score, he wanted to win. Even though they all knew there would be another game after this, and another game after that, until Mr. Lucchino finally told them to go wait out front for their parents.

When it was game point, Ned Hancock always played like he was playing for the championship of something, even if it was just the next time down the court.

Ned was a small forward, even though he wasn't small. He was tall enough to play center and a good enough shooter to play shooting guard. If he wanted to play point guard, he would have been better at handling and distributing the ball than Pedro was.

But he played forward. Point forward—that's the way Pedro thought of him, like they had two point guards in the game at the same time when they were on the same team.

Ned was a point *everything*, really.

Mr. Everything, that's what he was in basketball, and in their school, where he was the best student among the boys. He was even about to get elected president of Vernon Middle.

Forget about president of Vernon Middle, it was as if Ned was the mayor of all the kids their age in Vernon.

Before Ned inbounded the ball, he bent down to tie his sneakers, just as a way of buying a little time. As he did, he said to Pedro, "Let's run a high pick-and-roll. You and me. Just without the roll."

"Could you try that again in plain English?" Pedro said.

Ned did.

Pedro smiled as he began dribbling up the court.

Joe Sutter, the best rebounder in their grade and Pedro's best bud, was also on their team. Pedro wasn't worried about Joe getting in the way, because even though Joe didn't say much, he also didn't miss much. Sometimes he had a way of reading Pedro's mind, in a basketball game, a soccer game, or even in a video game.

Jeff Harmon—Ned's best bud—was guarding Pedro.

"Watch out for a trick play," Jeff called out. "I saw them talking down there."

Pedro was past half-court now, holding up a fist, which everybody on both teams knew meant absolutely nothing.

"Very funny," Jeff said.

No, Pedro thought, *just plain fun.*

This was always the best of it for him, in any sport, when he could see a play inside his head and was about to make it happen.

As soon as he began dribbling to his right, Joe cleared out of there and ran to the other side of the court. Like he just knew it was going to be a two-man game now—Ned and Pedro—the same way it had been so many times last season on the fifth-grade town team.

As soon as Joe cleared out, Ned came running up to what the announcers on television liked to call the "foul line extended," and set a monster pick on Jeff Harmon, who had been sliding to his left as he guarded Pedro. Jeff may have been Ned's bud, but it didn't help him now on game point, because when he ran into Ned's pick, nobody having called it out, Pedro could actually hear the air come out of him like it was coming out of a balloon.

Jeff was still sure he knew what was coming.

"Pick-and-roll!" he said, gasping for breath. "I've got Ned."

He stayed home on Ned. Bobby Murray left Ned now and picked up Pedro. And they would have had the play covered if Ned had kept going toward the basket, the way you were supposed to on the kind of pick-and-roll play they had been using all game long.

Only Ned, instead of cutting toward the basket, popped out a couple of steps *away* from it.

And instead of trying to beat Bobby Murray off the dribble, Pedro suddenly pulled up, too, spun and put the ball over his head and whipped a two-hand pass, hard, over to Ned.

The ball barely seemed to touch Ned's hands before it changed direction and came right back at Pedro.

It was just enough to make Jeff Harmon turn his head. As soon as he did, Ned was gone.

The only thing missing was that *whoosh* you got in a superhero movie when Spidey or the Silver Surfer or one of those guys was there and gone.

Pedro didn't even bother catching the ball, just tap-passed it back to Ned over Jeff's head and over the rest of the defense, a sweet little floater of a pass, almost like they were playing volleyball on the beach and he was setting Ned up for a spike.

Ned didn't spike it. He just caught the ball and laid it up in one motion. Ballgame.

Even a couple of the guys on defense put their hands together.

So did Mr. Lucchino, standing in the open gym door.

Pedro stood in the exact same spot from where he'd delivered the pass and watched as Ned, as usual, got high-fives all around. Joe once said that you didn't need one of those GPS guidance gizmos from your parents' car to locate Ned Hancock—just the sound of applause.

Everybody was acting as if Ned had somehow passed the ball to himself.

Pedro didn't care. If you played with Ned you knew it was his game, and you were just playing in it. It had pretty much been that way since they'd first become teammates, and Pedro accepted it. He was a point guard and he always remembered something he'd read once from a famous coach named Larry Brown, who said that the only stat that mattered for a point guard was the final score—whether or not his team had won the game, not how many points and assists he had.

Their team had won, and that was enough for Pedro. That and the satisfaction of making that pass, delivering that baby like it was the afternoon mail.

Joe Sutter, when he did talk, liked to say that the best thing about his buddy Pedro was that he knew who he was. He never needed to be a star, on any team he'd ever played for. He didn't need to put himself out there, to say to everybody, *Hey, look at me.*

He just wanted to win the game.